The Order of the Pure Moon Reflected in Water

The Order of the Pure Moon Reflected in Water

ZEN CHO

A TOM DOHERTY ASSOCIATES BOOK · NEW YORK

THE ORDER OF THE PURE MOON REFLECTED IN WATER

Copyright © 2020 by Zen Cho

All rights reserved.

Edited by Jonathan Strahan

Designed by Greg Collins

A Tor.com Book
Published by Tom Doherty Associates
120 Broadway
New York, NY 10271

www.tor.com

Tor® is a registered trademark of Macmillan Publishing Group, LLC.

The Library of Congress Cataloging-in-Publication Data is available upon request.

ISBN 978-1-250-26925-6 (hardcover)
ISBN 978-1-250-26924-9 (ebook)

Our books may be purchased in bulk for promotional, educational, or business use. Please contact your local bookseller or the Macmillan Corporate and Premium Sales Department at 1-800-221-7945, extension 5442, or by email at MacmillanSpecialMarkets@macmillan.com.

First Edition: June 2020

Printed in the United States of America

0 9 8 7 6 5 4 3 2 1

To Rae

The
Order
of the
Pure Moon
Reflected
in Water

There was a brief lull in the general chatter when the bandit walked into the coffeehouse.

This was not because of the knife at his hip or his dusty attire, suggestive of a life spent in the jungle. It was not the first time Weng Wah Coffeehouse had seen a bandit and it would not be the last.

The coffeehouse was the kind of establishment common in any town with more than two Tang people. The floors were tiled and of dubious cleanliness. A painting of a herd of horses dominated the green walls. Below the horses were posters advertising beverages of various types.

The tables were sticky, the waiters loud and the chairs rickety.

And as in any town on the peninsula with more than two Tang people, everyone there was used to bandits. It was of course safest to avoid bandits, but since most looked like ordinary people—indeed, if you were unlucky, some of them were your cousin, your uncle, your brother—this was not always possible.

This bandit did not look like anyone's brother. His chief characteristic, and what made everyone fall silent for an unintended moment, was his extreme beauty. His skin was as pure as jade; his eyes and eyebrows were like ink; his dark hair, bound in a queue, was like silk; and his face was like the full moon among clouds.

The waiter stood gaping at him. The bandit had to gesture pointedly at the table before Ah Kheng leapt into action with a grubby cloth.

"You have soya bean?" said the bandit. "I'll have it hot and sweet."

The chatter resumed, though there was a new frisson to it. It was mid-morning, so the worst of the breakfast rush had subsided, but there were still plenty of customers. Some departed discreetly, but others stayed, stealing glances at the bandit.

The bandit was used to surreptitious scrutiny and did not let it bother him. He smiled enchantingly at Ah Kheng when his drink arrived, but otherwise paid no attention to anyone else. He was busy reading the poster pinned above his table.

It was one of the few posters that did not extol the delights of beer or umbra juice. Instead, it depicted the morose faces of five men. Beneath these, a calligrapher had inscribed:

By the order of the Protector, guardian of all that lies between the Straits and the Southern Seas, any sighting of these bandits is to be reported to the Protectorate at once. Anyone found to have given these criminals succour will be punished.

The bandit was gazing so intently at the wanted men that he did not appear to notice the quarrel brewing between a waitress and the customer at the next table. He didn't stir even when the customer shouted:

"Useless girl, did you think I wouldn't notice your jampi?"

The observers could never agree on what happened next. Some vowed the cup of tea jumped into the air of its own accord. But of course this was not possible. The waitress must have thrown it at the shouting customer. In any case, the man smacked it away. It went flying, hurtling towards the back of the bandit's head.

The bandit leaned out of the way and watched as tea drenched the poster. The cup clattered onto his table, rolling to a stop.

"What's going on?" cried the owner of the coffeehouse, rushing out of the kitchen.

He took in the situation in one horrified glance. The waitress was looking defiant, the customer irate. The latter wore once-rich robes that had seen better days. There was a gap in his front teeth where, perhaps, a gold tooth had once been.

The coffeehouse owner snapped at the waitress, "What did you do?"

The customer was red-faced. "This girl tried to hex me! You don't try to deny. I know what magic smells like!"

"I didn't try to deny also," said the waitress, with an injured air.

She was probably not much younger than the bandit, but her bald head gave her an innocent look. She was pretty enough that she did not suffer from adopting the grooming standards of the monastic orders. To look at her was to wonder why all women did not shave their heads.

She gave the coffeehouse owner a look of appeal, but he was unmoved.

"You hexed a customer?" he roared. He smacked her on the side of the head.

"I didn't say that, Mr Aw," protested the waitress, rubbing her head. "I just said I didn't deny only."

"What kind of establishment is this, hiring witches to

serve people?" said the customer. "Normal people are too expensive, is it?"

Mr Aw looked anxious. "Sir, please . . ."

The bandit's eyebrow twitched. He sighed and turned around.

"It's not the girl's fault," he said. "Uncle started it." He gestured at the angry customer.

"That sounds highly unlikely!" said Mr Aw.

"Who are you to say?" said the irate customer to the bandit. "You didn't even see what was happening!"

"I heard you pinch the other waiter's ass," said the bandit, bored. "It's not even that good an ass. Shouldn't you be more discriminating when you harass people?"

"That's so rude," said the waitress indignantly. "Ah Kheng, you don't listen to him! You have a very nice ass!"

Ah Kheng had vanished, but his voice drifted out from the kitchen: "Please stop talking about my ass."

"Ah, sorry," said the bandit. He looked mildly embarrassed. "If I knew you were there, I wouldn't have commented on your ass." He turned to the irate customer. "Uncle, give face to this gentleman—what's your name?"

"Mr Aw," said Mr Aw.

"Mr Aw is just trying to run his business," said the bandit to the customer. "It's hard to make a living these days. We Tang people must try to get along."

He reached into his robe and drew out a woven purse,

which he threw at the coffeehouse owner. Mr Aw caught it with the neatness of a man who would know the jingling of cash at fifty paces. He opened the purse while the waitress peered over his shoulder. Their eyes widened.

"A thank you for maintaining the peace in your coffeehouse," said the bandit. He nodded at the waitress. "And for being a benevolent employer."

He turned back to his study of the poster with the air of one washing his hands of the matter.

"Are you going to—you're just going to take a bribe right in front of me?" said the irate customer.

"Sir could have half?" said Mr Aw.

"I don't want half," said the customer. "I want justice!"

"In these times justice is hard to get," said the waitress sagely. "Better you take the money, sir. Maybe you cannot afford a new tooth, but you can definitely buy new clothes."

"You . . . !"

There was a tearing noise from the bandit's table. They fell quiet, but the bandit was only folding the poster delicately and putting it into his robe. He stood up.

"Ah, sir," said Mr Aw. "Sorry, but I have to keep that sign, sir. I'll get in trouble if the mata see I don't have it."

"Difficult," agreed the bandit. "But what can I do? I can't read it here. That fellow is too noisy. I cannot focus."

He jerked his head towards the irate customer, who turned purple.

"Who asked you to be a busybody?" said the customer.

"Uncle, you're being very troublesome," said the bandit. "Look, you've chased away all of Mr Aw's customers already. Why don't you leave with me?

"I don't mean go away together," he clarified. "I mean leave here at the same time, separately. Let the lady be. Heaven will punish her if she is wrong."

"That's right," said the waitress, but the customer did not agree.

"'Lady'!" he snorted. "This girl is a useless slut."

"Actually, I'm a nun," said the waitress, pointing at her bald head. "So, literally the opposite of a slut!"

"Oh, shut up," growled the customer. He backhanded her. The waitress fell back, looking more startled than frightened.

The bandit sighed. "That wasn't very gentlemanly."

"Nobody asked you, pretty boy!" snapped the customer.

The bandit's forehead furrowed. "Is that the best insult you can offer? Never mind."

There weren't many witnesses left to quarrel about what happened next. But as he peeked out from the kitchen, Ah Kheng saw the bandit take the customer's feet out from under him and pin him up against the wall. It was done in one fluid movement from start to finish.

"Now," said the bandit.

But there was more to the customer than his appearance indicated. He spat in the bandit's face. As the bandit recoiled, the customer's hand moved to his side. Metal gleamed between their bodies.

"Brother, watch out!" cried Ah Kheng, but he needn't have worried about the bandit. The bandit slipped the customer's dagger out of his hand, whistling when he got a closer look at it.

"This is a nice keris!" The bandit wiped his face against his sleeve. "Where did you get it from? Keris have souls, you know. It's bad luck to steal one if your spirit is not strong."

"Shut up, shut up, shut up!" screamed the customer. "Little brother, come to me!" He launched himself at the bandit.

The waitress was bouncing on the soles of her feet, looking for a gap between the fighters, when a strong grip seized her by both arms, immobilising her. She looked up into the customer's face.

She looked back at the fighting men. The bandit was flinging the customer into a stack of chairs.

A man could not be in two places at once. Unless . . .

"Black magic!" she gasped. "No wonder he's so fast to accuse people of jampi."

"You're going to learn to respect people," growled the irate customer's duplicate, hoisting her into the air.

"What about your master?" said the waitress. "Respect goes two ways. When's *he* going to learn to respect people?"

Before the duplicate could answer, a chair slammed into the back of its head. Its eyes rolled up and it slumped.

The waitress managed to wriggle out of its grasp before it collapsed with a thud that shook the floor.

She looked reproachfully at the man holding the chair. "Couldn't you wait? I wanted to know what it was going to say."

"You're welcome," said the man. He set down the chair and looked past her at the fight.

Mr Aw had retreated to the kitchen, where he and Ah Kheng could be seen goggling while the bandit and the disgruntled customer threw each other around.

The newcomer sighed. It was clear he, too, was a bandit. Like the first bandit, he had an outlaw's air and wore clothes that had seen a great deal of contact with the elements, but he was not at all beautiful. If the first bandit was a porcelain vase, this one was an everyday clay vessel, suitable for holding water or budu or rice wine, as the occasion demanded. He was of medium height, dark for a Tang person and sturdily made. His long hair was bound into a tail at the top of his head, and he had a parang strapped across his back.

"Do I want to know what happened here?" he said.

"Your sworn brother is defending my honour," explained the waitress. "It's very nice of him. Of course, now I will definitely lose my job. But I'm sure his intentions are good."

The clay-vessel bandit looked at her. "You're a devotee of the Pure Moon Reflected in Water."

The waitress grinned. "How could you tell?"

The clay-vessel bandit shook his head. "This Ah Lau is always doing unnecessary things." He produced a small bag from his robes, pouring out a generous number of copper coins onto his palm and holding them out to the waitress. "For your lost job."

"You bandits must be doing well," said the waitress, impressed.

The clay-vessel bandit put the bag back into his robe. "You should go."

"What are you going to do, brother?"

"Nothing you should see," said the clay-vessel bandit.

"But I want to—"

"Go."

The waitress looked mutinous, but he didn't look at her, and after a moment she went.

In fact, the clay-vessel bandit did not do anything spectacular. That would not have been his style. He stumped over to the fighters, undaunted by the broken-off chair legs, plates with noodles still on them and soiled cutlery flying through the air. As he approached, the first bandit ducked and the customer hauled off, preparing to punch him. The clay-vessel bandit grabbed the customer's arm and said:

"You can choose to stop fighting, or I can stop you. It's up to you."

"Eat shit, bastard!"

The clay-vessel bandit shrugged. He jabbed the customer in the neck with two fingers and watched dispassionately as the man crumpled to the floor.

The first bandit rose, rolling his shoulders and cracking his neck. "I wish you'd teach me how to do that, Ah Sang."

The clay-vessel bandit was known as Tet Sang to his friends. "You'd only do useless things with it," he said. He gave the devastation around them a pointed look. "What are you going to say to the owner?"

"I paid him already," said the first bandit, but he wasn't interested in Mr Aw's feelings. He fumbled in his robe, taking out the poster. "Look. What do you think?"

Tet Sang read the heading aloud: "*Notice regarding the incorrigible criminals, enemies of the Protectorate, Lau Fung Cheung and his men.*" His face darkened. "It was only a matter of time before we started drawing attention, I suppose."

"At least it's free advertising," said the first bandit, who happened to be Lau Fung Cheung. "Maybe we'll get new business."

"It's one thing to be known as men willing to bend the law," said Tet Sang. "But nobody wants to hire *wanted criminals*." He studied the portraits, his head to one side. "You're better-looking in real life. The artist must be somebody's cousin."

Extraordinarily, Lau Fung Cheung blushed.

"Are you done?" said Tet Sang. "Can we go?"

"I haven't finished my drink," said Fung Cheung. His table and soya bean milk had somehow survived the battle. He picked up his glass and sipped from it. He made a face. "Cold already."

His sworn brother rolled his eyes. Mr Aw, lurking behind the counter, yelped and ducked when their eyes met.

"Drink up," said Tet Sang. "I'll settle the bill."

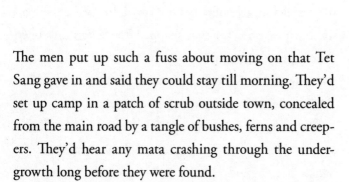

The men put up such a fuss about moving on that Tet Sang gave in and said they could stay till morning. They'd set up camp in a patch of scrub outside town, concealed from the main road by a tangle of bushes, ferns and creepers. They'd hear any mata crashing through the undergrowth long before they were found.

Still, if Tet Sang were an enthusiastic Protectorate official on the hunt for bandits, this was the first place he would look. An ambush by the authorities was the last thing they needed right now, with the goods they were carrying. He was restless all evening, jumping at every hoot of a passing owl.

"You're like an old woman," said Fung Cheung, the originating cause of all this anxiety. "Don't worry so much. That Mr Aw is not stupid; he won't be making a report. Even if he does, they won't send out the mata for a brawl in a coffeehouse."

Fung Cheung must have known he was speaking nonsense. The Protectorate would send out their forces at the merest whiff of bandits, and any trouble at a Tang-run coffeehouse would be presumed to involve bandits. Tet Sang gave him a look but only said:

"I'm not worried. I'm on my guard. That's different."

There was always someone on watch at night, but that night it was Ah Hin, who'd had a little too much beer at dinner. It was a wonder his snoring didn't wake them all up, but it wasn't that that snapped Tet Sang's eyes open shortly after midnight.

He was fully awake in a moment. He threw himself on the intruder, rolling them onto their back.

The waitress from Weng Wah Coffeehouse stifled a squeak. Her alarm changed to relief when she saw Tet Sang's face.

"It's you, brother!" she said, pleased. "I was wondering which one you were. You all look the same in the dark."

The others stirred. Ah Hin leapt up, shouting:

"Big Brother! Intruder! Fire! Attack!"

Fung Cheung was on his feet, his knife at the ready. "Ah Sang, you caught him? Who is it?"

Tet Sang sat back on his haunches, letting the waitress go. She dusted herself off fastidiously.

"Nobody," said Tet Sang. "Just a woman."

Someone lit a torch and the scene blossomed into clarity—the groggy men rubbing their eyes and reaching for their weapons; the bald woman with her calm, infuriating smile.

"A nun," the waitress corrected him. "A votary of the Order of the Pure Moon Reflected in Water."

This was for the benefit of their audience. Tet Sang already knew it, and from the gleam in the waitress's eye, she hadn't forgotten this.

"You're the girl from the coffeehouse," said Fung Cheung.

"What's your name?" said Tet Sang.

The waitress folded her hands. "At my tokong they called me Nirodha."

Tet Sang raised an eyebrow. "And your actual name?"

The waitress held his eyes for half a second before her gaze faltered. "My birth name was Guet Imm."

Ah Hin had digested the implications of the waitress being a follower of the Pure Moon.

"That girl is a witch!" he said. "Must be she enchanted me, that's why I fell asleep!"

Suspicious muttering rose from the group like a bad smell.

"Did you enchant Ah Hin?" said Tet Sang.

Guet Imm looked injured. "No! Brother was already sleeping when I came. He looked tired, so I tried not to wake him up. I was looking for you, brother."

"What for?"

"You're the one I know," explained Guet Imm.

Tet Sang jerked his head towards Fung Cheung. "You know him."

"Yes, but you're the one I trust," said Guet Imm.

"Because of you, I fought that guy!" said Fung Cheung, offended.

"Yeah," said Guet Imm apologetically. "Sorry, brother. But because of your fight, Mr Aw fired me."

"He would have fired you anyway. You cannot go around hexing customers and expect to keep your job. It's bad customer service."

"He might have changed his mind before you got involved," argued Guet Imm. "Anyway, this brother was actually helpful." She gestured at Tet Sang. "He gave me money."

"He did?" said Fung Cheung. He clapped Tet Sang on the back, delighted. "Ah Sang, you didn't say! When you're always scolding me for being too generous! All the more we shouldn't worry. That coffeehouse earnt a lot of money today. It would be too ungrateful if they put the mata on us after all that."

"I'm not at the coffeehouse anymore," said Guet Imm. "I *said* they let me go."

"Big Brother," said Ah Hin urgently, "what about the witch's jampi?"

But he'd lost his moment. Fung Cheung would have forgiven the nun much worse for such ammunition against Tet Sang as she'd given him.

"Come on, Ah Hin, you don't need this sister's jampi to fall asleep on watch," said Fung Cheung. "You've done it so many times, must be you offended some spirit. We better take you to visit a sinseh in the next town, see if he can cure you."

Amid the ensuing merriment at Ah Hin's expense, Tet Sang said to the nun, "I gave you the money so you would go away. What happened to it?"

Guet Imm held up a soft black thing like the hide of a small animal. It turned out to be a wig. "I bought this so I'm not so conspicuous. It fell off when you jumped on me."

She put it on her head. The effect was singularly unconvincing.

"I still have the rest of the money," she added. "I thought of getting pots and pans, maybe some cooking chopsticks. But I wasn't sure what you all had already."

"Huh?" said Tet Sang.

"Oh, I'm joining you all," said Guet Imm, wide-eyed. "Didn't I say already?"

"You definitely did not say that!"

Guet Imm looked piteous. "But I don't have anywhere

else to go. Brother"—she meant Fung Cheung—"caused me to lose my job." Another thought struck her. "And you saved my life! That's two reasons why you have to look after me now."

Tet Sang's brow furrowed. "Wait, how does that even—"

"Don't worry, brother. I won't be a burden. I'll make myself useful. I learnt how to cook at the coffeehouse. And," the nun added, with rather more confidence, "I'm great at cleaning!"

"We're roving contractors," said Tet Sang. "We have *nothing to clean.*"

"Oh, I wouldn't say that," said Guet Imm, looking at Tet Sang's clothes in an unflattering way. "Contractors, huh? I thought you were bandits. What kind of contract work do you do? Building houses, stuff like that?"

"More 'stuff like that,'" said Fung Cheung. It was evident the nun amused him.

This was a bad sign. Fung Cheung would do anything for a laugh. Tet Sang glared at him, but before he could say anything, Ah Boon intervened.

"Maybe it's not such a bad idea, Big Brother," he said to Fung Cheung. "It gets boring, just us men. A woman in the group could contribute something different. She says she'll make herself useful. I'm sure she can help us out—do more than cooking and cleaning. You won't mind being kind to us, right, little sister?"

Ah Boon chucked the nun under her chin. It was like

watching an idiot child pull a tiger's tail. Tet Sang leant back.

But Guet Imm kept her hands in her lap. She looked puzzled, but after a moment, her face cleared.

"Oh, you mean sex!" she said. "Would you want me to have sex with you?"

"No!" said Tet Sang.

"Yes?" said Ah Boon.

"Maybe," said Fung Cheung.

Guet Imm considered it. "I can do that. I've never done it before, but it can't be difficult, right? Even cats and dogs know how to do.

"Of course," she added, "as a devotee of the Pure Moon, I vowed when I first shaved my head that I would have no profane intercourse with men. If I break my vow to the deity, I must make sure to cleanse myself afterwards. I would need to make a sacrifice each time."

"We're very open in this company," said Fung Cheung. "Everyone can practise their religion, no problem. You ask Rimau; we never eat pork."

"Correct," said Rimau, who had fallen asleep last night after three gourds of beer.

"She means," said Tet Sang, "she'd have to chop off the dick of any man she fucked."

"That's right," said Guet Imm, approving of his acuity. "You're very clever about our doctrine, brother! Are you a follower also?"

"There was a tokong of the Pure Moon in the town where I grew up," said Tet Sang.

"Chop off our *dicks*?" said Ah Boon.

"It's how I would wash out the sin," explained Guet Imm. "Using the men's blood. Strictly, my teacher would say I must do the cleansing even if I didn't go so far as to have the profane intercourse. Even thinking of betraying my vows is enough! If we are being strict, I should make the sacrifice now you've raised the subject."

She directed a speculative look at Ah Boon's crotch but shook her head. "But I think that's too rigid. Let's see what happens. I am homeless, I have nowhere to go. I'm sure the deity will close one eye on this occasion.

"Of course, if she doesn't, we'll soon find out," she said brightly. "The deity is amazing. There was one time this novice at my tokong stole the joss sticks to eat—she was always a bit weird—and before anyone even found out, her father's house burnt down! The family lost everything."

"We can't take her," said Ah Boon to Fung Cheung.

But Tet Sang had read the signs right. Fung Cheung hadn't been that interested in the sex. He'd already made up his mind. He replied:

"You may enjoy Ah Yee's cooking, but I'm getting fed up."

"Big Brother, if you don't want me to cook, I don't have to do it," said Ah Yee in a throbbing voice.

"Don't be stupid," said Tet Sang. "Your food is disgusting, but nobody else can do it."

"At least *you* appreciate me, Second Brother!"

Tet Sang turned to the nun. "This is ridiculous. You can't come with us. Take your money, get out of here and find another job."

He grabbed her arm, intending to escort her out of their camp, but it was like trying to shift a boulder. Guet Imm wouldn't budge. She remained seated, cross-legged like a statue of the Pure Moon in repose.

She shook off Tet Sang's hand with rather less effort than it would take to bat away a fly. "No."

Tet Sang looked at his hand, then at her. "No?"

"You're not the boss," said Guet Imm. She nodded at Fung Cheung. "Brother is the boss. I knew it straight away, from the nobility of his countenance."

"I was the helpful one," Tet Sang reminded her. "The one who gave you money, remember? You said you didn't trust Ah Lau."

"I trust him now," said Guet Imm. "Before, I admit I misunderstood him. I thought, who is this busybody fellow, poking his nose into other people's business? Nobody asked him to beat up that guy also. Because he wants to show off, I must lose my job.

"But now I see I was wrong. This encounter has shown me his true character. Brother is like a knight-errant of the olden days, rescuing people from corrupt authority. His heart is like beaten gold, as beautiful as his face."

She gazed at Fung Cheung, her eyes shining.

Tet Sang's heart fell. Fung Cheung loved being gazed at adoringly—ideally by handsome young men, but a pretty woman would do in a pinch.

Guet Imm reached out a reverent hand, touching Fung Cheung's shin.

"Brother," she said, "I know you won't let me down!"

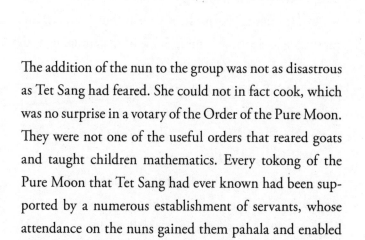

The addition of the nun to the group was not as disastrous
as Tet Sang had feared. She could not in fact cook, which
was no surprise in a votary of the Order of the Pure Moon.
They were not one of the useful orders that reared goats
and taught children mathematics. Every tokong of the
Pure Moon that Tet Sang had ever known had been supported by a numerous establishment of servants, whose
attendance on the nuns gained them pahala and enabled
the nuns to devote their days exclusively to study, meditation and self-cultivation.

To be fair to Guet Imm, she was less useless than most
Pure Moon devotees. She managed to part the men from

their filthy clothes and launder them, in the teeth of the men's appalled resistance. She also proved handy with a needle, skilled at leech removal, and knowledgeable about where to find herbs to keep off the mosquitoes.

Even when the group gave in to the inevitable and admitted that Ah Yee must take over cooking duties again if they were not all to be poisoned, there was no suggestion of getting rid of the nun. They had all got used to itching less.

"And you all smell better now," said Guet Imm. "Well done!"

The group walked in the evenings and mornings, stopping to rest late at night and in the dull intolerable heat of the afternoons. At most, they had four hours of uninterrupted sleep at any time. Some of the group, used to waking in the day and sleeping at night, had found it hard to get used to this when they first joined, but the pattern of their days was not unlike that adopted by the monastic orders, and it did not seem to trouble Guet Imm. She travelled well and did not complain of discomfort, so Tet Sang would not have known that she felt any, had he not noticed her stealing away from the group one night.

After a moment's reflection, he followed her. They had pitched camp in an abandoned plantation that was slowly being retaken by the jungle. There was more than one kind of danger here, for Guet Imm as much as for the group.

He found her sitting on a log with her shoes off, rinsing her feet with water from a stream. She had not brought a torch with her, but Tet Sang was not surprised that she had not needed it to navigate the scrub in the dark.

He had not made a sound, but she looked up suddenly, her face a pale oval in the moonlight filtering through the canopy.

Tet Sang had all the bandit's fabled ability to move in the forest without being detected. He was fairly sure he had done nothing to betray his presence, but still he shrank behind a tree.

"What are you doing here, brother?" said the nun. For once, she sounded annoyed.

Tet Sang stepped out of the shadows.

"What's wrong with your leg?" he said.

But now he could see the state of her feet—blistered and rubbed raw from walking. She shifted away from Tet Sang, bending to pat her feet dry. A wince briefly displaced her frown.

"You should call Ah Boon to look at that," said Tet Sang, embarrassed. "He can give you medicine. He used to look after people's cows."

"That's some recommendation," said Guet Imm. "I'm okay. It's a small thing only. I'm not used to walking so much, but my feet will toughen up."

Tet Sang knew he should leave her alone. Nobody had

asked her to come along. If her feet hurt, it was her own fault.

"I thought the votaries of the Pure Moon were taught healing arts," he said. "What do you call it? 'Shaping the air'?"

"Very good!" said Guet Imm snappishly. "You know a lot, brother, but you don't know everything. We can't use the deity's gifts for selfish purposes. The five fingers of her hand are only to benefit other people."

"Healing your feet is to benefit us," said Tet Sang. "We have an appointment to get to. You have to keep up. We can't afford to get slowed down."

Guet Imm's gaze was steely.

"You don't need to worry, brother," she said. "I'll keep up."

She sat there with her head held high, her eyes on his, until he went away.

He did not let the incident bother him, though they were taking longer than they should to get to Sungai Tombak, where they were to make delivery of the goods. After the hue and cry Fung Cheung had raised at the last town, Tet Sang had insisted on taking a circuitous route, avoiding their usual haunts.

The Protectorate's posters might not have borne a very good likeness of Fung Cheung and his men, but they had got the names and descriptions more or less right. You never knew whether a chancer hoping for a reward might turn them in. These were uncertain times, and hunger a powerful incentive even for the faint-hearted.

It was only prudent to go the long way round. Tet Sang refused to feel guilty about it. Guet Imm was evidently determined not to be pitied, anyway. Her gait never faltered during the day, though she still crept away in the evenings.

She made it easier not to feel sorry for her by refusing to talk to him for a time, while taking pains to be especially nice to everyone else. She struck up a particular friendship with Ah Hin, who had always had urgings towards religion.

"If not for my mother, I would have joined an order," he was wont to say wistfully. "But how to support her as a monk? Begging and chanting prayers, maybe you can get rice for yourself, but not for your family. Life could have been different. I would have been educated if I followed a god."

Being illiterate, he had restricted his religious endeavours to wasting his hard-earned share of the group's earnings on donations to the religious orders and buying charms and trinkets from monks. To nuns, he had never paid attention before. But after Guet Imm had accompanied them for some time, Ah Hin realised that she did not rise earlier than everyone else to sit, cross-legged and unmoving with her eyes shut, for no reason.

"Sister Guet Imm," he said after he had watched her, rapt, for half an hour, "you were meditating!"

Guet Imm looked puzzled. "Yes? It's one of the five fingers of the deity's hand. Emptying the gourd—meditation—is the first finger, the most fundamental. Everything follows from that. Filling the gourd, planting seeds . . ."

Ah Hin wasn't listening. Excited, he rummaged through his possessions and produced a small crumpled booklet, printed in red ink.

"The Abbot gave me this at the last tokong we passed. The last tokong that was still standing," he corrected himself. "They followed a different deity, but . . . can you read it to me, sister?"

Guet Imm read out the title: "*Scriptures of the Baby God.*" She flipped through the tract, nodding.

Her prohibition on profane intercourse with men aside, the Pure Moon was not a jealous goddess. Tet Sang had once known a votary of her Order who had snuck out every fifth-day to make offerings at other houses of worship—those dedicated to the gods of the Malayu and the Damilans as well as the Tang pantheon. She even went to the Protectorate's churches: "Safer to keep all the gods happy," she'd said pragmatically.

"Rather than I read to you," said Guet Imm, "isn't it better if I teach you how to read yourself?"

"Oh, no," said Ah Hin, taken aback. "I'm not clever, sister. I went to school one whole year and I learnt how to gamble only."

"Doesn't matter whether you're clever or not," said Guet Imm. "With the deity's help, all things can be done."

She appropriated one of the group's torches and attended patiently to Ah Hin every evening as he read aloud, stumbling over the red words. The tract recounted the adventures of a boy god, a troublesome infant who spent more time subduing dragons and taming seas than preaching about ethics or spiritual cultivation.

It was a good story, with plenty of fighting. The group found the Baby God far more sympathetic than they would have found the Pure Moon. Their complaints about Guet Imm's annexation of the torch died down, and Ah Hin's education was stimulated by the brothers' objections to his halting pace.

Tet Sang was the one member of the group who did not enjoy their story-time sessions. Perhaps to the others it was natural to see a woman with her head bent, her nape deceptively vulnerable and her lashes casting shadows on her cheeks, as she devoted herself to a man. No doubt the scene recalled memories of the mothers, sisters, aunts and cousins who had once tended to them.

Tet Sang had come to the group with a different set of memories. He knew how dangerous it could be to assume that either women or mystics were harmless.

There was no reason to worry, he told himself. It was not a good time for Tang religious orders, and the Order of the Pure Moon had suffered as much as the others from the Protectorate's purges. Without her tokong, the nun depended on the group for her livelihood. She would do nothing to jeopardize that.

Still, he thought it his duty to warn Ah Hin.

"Better be careful around that nun," Tet Sang said one morning. "You don't know what her intentions are."

Ah Hin gave him a wounded look. "You're always so suspicious, brother. Why don't you like Sister Guet Imm?"

"It's been two weeks," said Tet Sang. "We don't know anything about where she's from or what she's done. Just because she's a religious doesn't mean she's sincere. You know what they say about devotees of the Pure Moon." There were rumours about the powers the deity granted her followers, and the wise were cautious where magic was concerned.

Of course, the wise also did not tend to become roving contractors.

"I never thought you of all people would be prejudiced," said Ah Hin reproachfully.

"You're the one who called her a witch!"

"I didn't know sister then," said Ah Hin. "It's not right to suspect people because of their past. It's like if we didn't trust Ah Yee because he used to rob people's houses."

"We *didn't* trust Ah Yee! He wasn't allowed to keep watch by himself until he was with us for more than a year."

"You sound like a mata," said Ah Hin, ignoring this.

"Talking bad about the tokong, saying the orders are conspiring with bandits. Shouldn't we of all people sympathize with the monks and nuns? We also are misunderstood."

If Tet Sang hadn't known better, he would've thought Guet Imm had bewitched the group. They all liked her now. Even Ah Boon had got over his pique about the fact that she would only sleep with him if she could castrate him afterwards. Tet Sang wasn't sure how she'd won him over, until he saw Guet Imm showing Ah Boon some herbs she was drying over a fire.

"Very good for all kinds of things," she said. "You know when you drink too much beer, the next day your head hurts? This is what you want."

"You know a lot, sister," said Ah Boon.

Guet Imm waved off the compliment. "This is nothing much. I'm not to say a real healer like you, brother!"

She looked up, smiling, and caught Tet Sang's eyes by accident. He glared at her.

She had the grace to look embarrassed. Any properly trained follower of the Pure Moon was bound to know more about the healing arts than Ah Boon. He had been apprenticed to a village healer for only two years before the war broke out.

But then Guet Imm raised her chin and eyebrows, as much as to say, *What are you going to do about it?* She turned her back on Tet Sang.

Since he did not enjoy being a bringer of ill tidings, Tet

Sang decided to keep his own counsel. It wasn't like he hadn't tried to warn the others. He had done his duty to the best of his ability. It was only a matter of time before something happened to make them regret taking her on. But till then, there was little reason for him to pick quarrels with the men on Guet Imm's account.

His patience was rewarded about as well as forbearance generally is. They were only a few days' walk from Sungai Tombak when he twisted his ankle on an uneven patch of road.

Ah Boon put a poultice on it and told him to keep walking. Tet Sang would have done this in any event, but the pain slowed him down, and in the course of the day, he drifted to the tail end of the group, where Ah Hin and Guet Imm were usually to be found—whispering like lovers, said the others. But this was teasing, meaning nothing. Even those who still harboured hopes of Guet Imm relaxing her policy on profane intercourse knew that Ah Hin had joined the group out of a hopeless passion for Fung Cheung.

Tet Sang didn't notice he had fallen behind at first. His attention was on maintaining mastery over his feeble body, which objected stridently to what he was doing. But then he heard his own name.

"I don't know why Brother Tet Sang hates me," Guet Imm was saying. "I didn't do anything to him also. I took his money, but he offered! Maybe I should pay him back. I shouldn't have bought the wig."

The wig had been retired from use by general agreement.

"You must give face to Second Brother," said Ah Hin's voice. "Usually he's not like this. He's worried about getting to Sungai Tombak. We're late already."

"But what's at Sungai Tombak?" said Guet Imm. "Why is it so important to get there?"

"We're making a delivery."

Out of the corner of his eye, Tet Sang saw Guet Imm nod sagely. "The sacks you all are carrying. Is it candu or bullion or what?"

"If we had candu, Big Brother would have smoked it all up already," said Ah Hin. "What is bullion?"

Ah Hin was impressed when Guet Imm explained.

"You think too much of us, sister," he said. "If we were at the level where we could transport bullion, we could all retire! The sacks inside are rice only. Hard to find high-quality rice these days. The merchants in Sungai Tombak will pay a good price for it. But the main delivery is not that."

Tet Sang cleared his throat, but he was too late. Ah Hin was already saying proudly:

"The main goods are in here!" He gestured at the pack on his back.

Tet Sang swallowed his interruption. If he kicked up a fuss now, that would only serve to make it obvious that there was something about the goods he'd rather Guet Imm didn't know.

"Really?" said Guet Imm, looking at Ah Hin's pack with new interest. "What is it?"

"Oh, very valuable goods," said Ah Hin, shaking his head. "Top secret. We're taking turns to carry."

For a gang of outlaws, Tet Sang thought bitterly, the brothers were remarkably trusting. Without even being prodded, Ah Hin went on:

"We're taking the rice because Big Brother wants a decoy. In case the mata catch us, they will think we are transporting black-market rice only. Hopefully, the Baby God will protect us from a raid," he added piously. "But even if the mata come and confiscate the rice, that is no problem so long as the real goods are safe." He patted the pack.

Guet Imm's eyes were as round as longan seeds. "What *are* the real goods?"

It seemed to strike Ah Hin for the first time that perhaps he should not be talking so much.

"Oh, ah," he said uncomfortably. "I shouldn't say. Big Brother wouldn't like it."

"Brother, you will kill me!" said Guet Imm. "I won't tell. Just a quick peek. You know you can trust me."

She was reaching out when Tet Sang caught her hand.

"You shouldn't touch people's things without asking," he said. "Didn't they teach you that at your tokong?"

He kept his eyes on Guet Imm until she lowered her hand.

"There was no such thing as *your things* or *my things*

at the tokong," she said, with an attempt at dignity. "The deity calls us to share. Anyway, I asked, didn't I, Brother Ah Hin?"

"I didn't hear Ah Hin say yes," said Tet Sang.

They both looked at Ah Hin. He went a delicate purple.

"Brother didn't mind, right?" said Guet Imm.

Even Ah Hin must have clocked by now that there was good reason Guet Imm of all people should not find out what they were carrying. He said wretchedly:

"It's my fault, sister. I shouldn't simply talk."

"I wouldn't give you away," said Guet Imm, hurt. "It's not like there's anybody I could tell also. Everybody I used to know is dead."

"There's Mr Aw at Weng Wah Coffeehouse," said Tet Sang. "You're here to make yourself useful, sister, not ask questions. If you don't like the rules, you can go back to the coffeehouse."

He limped away before either of the others could answer.

Ah Hin followed Tet Sang, silently offering his shoulder. After Tet Sang's first moment of indignation, he took the offered support. At least it got Ah Hin away from the nun.

"Sorry, Second Brother," muttered Ah Hin.

Tet Sang grunted.

The ensuing silence was tense, Ah Hin's shoulders rigid beneath Tet Sang's arm. He realised Ah Hin was looking for something more than he'd given.

"Don't worry," said Tet Sang. "I won't tell Ah Lau."

"That's not why I apologized," said Ah Hin, affronted. "I know you won't do me like that, brother!"

Again, Ah Hin was being too trusting. Tet Sang kept the strict word of his promise, but Fung Cheung was not stupid. When Tet Sang said they should keep a closer watch on the goods, Fung Cheung raised an eyebrow.

"You're scared Ah Hin will give us away?" he said. "I've been thinking he's getting too pious."

"Excuse me, do I look like a running dog?" said Tet Sang.

Fung Cheung rolled his eyes, but he asked no more questions.

Nothing was said to Ah Hin, but from then on, only Fung Cheung, Tet Sang, or Rimau—a childhood friend of Fung Cheung's and married to his sister, now dead— were allowed to bear the goods.

Tet Sang had bad dreams of the past whenever it was his turn, but did not complain. The new arrangement served his purpose. Besides, his capacity for enduring pain was something he had measured to the precise outer edge of its limits.

Sungai Tombak was a mining town strung across a river and surrounded by forested hills. The group set up camp by a waterfall some miles outside the town, while Ah Boon and Ah Wing were sent ahead to make contact with the people waiting for their deliveries.

They returned with good news. All was in order. The next day they would deliver the rice—and the other goods.

It would not be a bad place to off-load the nun as well, thought Tet Sang wistfully. Sungai Tombak was somewhat past its peak, worn down by the depredations of both the banditry and the Protectorate in the long-drawn-out war. But the wave of tin money had not wholly receded and the town was still prosperous. A clever, biddable girl could easily find work with a merchant's family there. It was true Guet Imm was not especially biddable, but she had enough native cunning to make up for that.

Tet Sang was too busy to raise the idea with her, however. That night, they were all occupied with preparations for the delivery. Guet Imm had to repeat herself before anyone took notice of her.

"I want to come along tomorrow," she said.

Fung Cheung was inspecting the sacks of rice. He looked up, frowning. "What?"

Guet Imm sat on her heels with her fists on her knees, looking as if she was going to launch into an obeisance at any moment. Her expression was nervous but determined. "I want to go into town."

"You heard the plan," said Fung Cheung.

Tet Sang, Rimau and Ah Boon were to bring the rice to a contact on the outskirts of town who ran a sundry shop as a front for her flourishing business trading in black-market products. From there, Tet Sang would go alone with the remaining goods to meet a representative of the buyer in the town centre. The rest of the group would make themselves scarce—visits to gambling dens, brothels, relatives and shrines alike had been banned.

"We're not here to be tourists," said Fung Cheung. "I am not going also, even though my Third Great-Aunt will kill me if she finds out I came to Sungai Tombak and didn't go to see her."

They'd agreed Fung Cheung was too memorable. There were Tang and Malayu men like Tet Sang, Ah Boon and Rimau in every town on the peninsula. Now that their robes were being washed regularly, they did not even need to source a fresh suit of clothes in order to look like ordinary men. People would look through them—but not Fung Cheung.

"We can't afford to draw attention to ourselves," he said.

"I won't draw attention," said Guet Imm. "I can wear my wig. Nobody will notice me."

"Everybody will notice you if you wear your wig," said Tet Sang. "What do you want to go to town for?"

Guet Imm was good at manipulation and appearing harmless when she was not, but at the end of the day, she was a nun and the product of her early training. Telling outright lies was not her forte.

"I want to buy soap," she said.

"We don't need soap," said Fung Cheung. He jerked his head at the others. "If you make them cleaner some more, they won't recognise themselves."

"I'll stay close to Brother Tet Sang," said Guet Imm. "I won't cause any trouble."

"You're being troublesome right now," said Fung Cheung.

Guet Imm looked anxious, but whatever it was that

drove her, it wouldn't let her drop the subject. She opened her mouth.

"What was that ointment you were telling Ah Boon about?" said Tet Sang before she could speak. "Good for joint pain."

For once, Guet Imm was slow on the uptake. She blinked. "The one to use for massage? It's called—"

"You forgot the name, sister," said Ah Boon quickly. "You couldn't tell me."

"But you know what the bottle looks like, right?" said Tet Sang.

Their meaning dawned on Guet Imm. "Yes! A brown bottle, with a red chop on the label."

"What does the chop look like?" said Fung Cheung suspiciously.

But Guet Imm had got her head in the game now. She turned limpid eyes on him. "I don't remember, brother. It might have been an axe. Or a flower. Or three legs joined together . . . not sure, but I'll know the ointment when I smell it. Most herbalists will sell."

"She might as well come with me," Tet Sang said to Fung Cheung. "I'm fed up with this ankle pain. She can go shopping while I settle our business."

It would have been hard to say whether Fung Cheung or Guet Imm was more surprised. Guet Imm was better at hiding it. She pasted her habitual serene smirk on her face.

"You're the one who's going," said Fung Cheung finally. "But how are you going to disguise her?"

"Why does she need a disguise? She's not on a wanted poster," said Tet Sang. He looked at Guet Imm. "You aren't, are you?"

The nun shook her head. "I never broke a law in my life, brother!"

"I doubt that," said Tet Sang drily. To Fung Cheung he said, "So long as she doesn't wear the wig, we'll be okay. There'll be other monks and nuns on the streets of Sungai Tombak. The only difference is she won't be begging for money."

"Okay," said Fung Cheung.

He glanced at the nun as though he wondered whether she'd put a jampi on Tet Sang. But Guet Imm paid no attention to Fung Cheung. She was gazing at Tet Sang, her brow creased.

———

Ah Boon and Rimau were content to wait at the sundry shop where they'd dropped off the rice while Tet Sang went into the town centre to deliver the valuables. Of course, they did not miss the opportunity to lecture Guet Imm hilariously about brothels.

"Make sure you pick a decent one, with clean girls! Don't let the madam cheat you!"

Tet Sang and Guet Imm left them drinking beer and playing cards with the sundry-shop owner.

For a time, Tet Sang and Guet Imm walked in silence, the nun stealing looks at Tet Sang while he pretended not to notice. They'd set out early that morning, when it was still dark, but now it was getting light, the rising sun turning the sky silver. Acres of rubber plantations and scrub unfolded on both sides of the road. Though the trees were recent arrivals, they might have been there forever—the silence of a much older forest breathed from them.

Guet Imm broke it, saying, "Thank you, brother."

Tet Sang did not bother feigning incomprehension. "So long as you find the ointment. I'm sick of being pummelled by Ah Boon like I'm a side of beef."

"He knows what the ointment is called," said Guet Imm. "I wrote it down for him. Ah Boon is educated—he went to school until twelve years old."

"I know."

Guet Imm gave him a sidelong look. "Why did you help me, brother?"

"Herbalists sell rags, right?" said Tet Sang. "You're going to get in trouble if you keep tearing off parts of your robe."

Menstruation was subject to no taboos in the Order of the Pure Moon, since it was an affliction most of the devotees shared. No doubt even the deity suffered from her monthly visitations. Guet Imm was more taken aback than embarrassed, and after a moment, even surprise was overtaken by outrage.

"But I was so careful!" she said. "I walked so far every day to find somewhere to wash the rags, so people wouldn't notice. I thought you all would mind!" She spoke with disgust at the wasted effort. "If I knew you didn't care, I wouldn't have tried to hide it. I only did it because I thought you all would be sensitive."

"Maybe the others would be sensitive. But they haven't realised," said Tet Sang. "You were careful." And the men were not observant when it came to these matters. Tet Sang knew from experience that they would miss far more obvious symptoms than Guet Imm had displayed. Either she was one of those happy persons whose periods gave them little trouble, or her stoicism over her blistered feet extended to cramps and cold sweats. She had shown no sign of enduring agonies.

Guet Imm eyed him suspiciously. "How did *you* know?"

"Herbs," said Tet Sang. "What else would you pick kacip fatimah for?" A new thought struck him. The cut of the votarial robes *was* very forgiving . . . "Unless you're pregnant?"

"No!" said Guet Imm, insulted. "Do I look like a vow-breaker to you, brother?"

"It's hard to follow the gods' rules in these times," said Tet Sang. "Not everybody can manage perfect virtue."

His tone was mild, but he intended it as a reprimand

and Guet Imm took his meaning. She went quiet, but she kept glancing at Tet Sang, until against his better judgment he said:

"What is it?"

"Nothing," said Guet Imm. Then: "You're more perceptive than you look, brother."

Tet Sang grunted. But as he had known would happen, Guet Imm took his question as an open invitation to talk about her feelings.

"All this time, I thought you hated me," she said.

Tet Sang felt there had been quite enough conversation already. But under the nun's expectant gaze, the words unspooled from him, almost without his volition. "I don't give money to people I hate."

"But you don't want me around."

"Sungai Tombak is a nice town," said Tet Sang. "Have you been here before?"

Guet Imm looked askance at this diversion, but she shook her head. "I haven't travelled much. My family gave me to the tokong when I was a baby, and after I entered seclusion, of course there was no chance."

"Seclusion?" Tet Sang had been avoiding eye contact, but he forgot himself and stared. "You were an anchorite?"

"Why is everybody so surprised by that?" said Guet Imm, displeased.

Tet Sang was reflecting on Guet Imm's mix of naiveté and cunning, the earthy but unswerving piety, and above all, the impression she gave of finding the society of others a delightful innovation. "Actually, it explains a lot."

"What's *that* supposed to mean?"

"The rich tin families here have a good relationship with the Protector," said Tet Sang. "So, they don't get bothered. People can still go on with their lives, not like some towns. You'll see when we get to the centre. You could get a job as a washerwoman or a healer."

"See, you don't want me around!" said Guet Imm. "Why not?"

"Why would I want you? Everybody else can carry and fight," said Tet Sang. "What do you contribute?"

"I'm charming, I'm helpful and I give your rough bandit lifestyle the much-needed touch of a woman."

Tet Sang snorted. "That's exactly what you're not giving. How many meals have you made for us? I mean," he said, as Guet Imm opened her mouth, "meals we can eat. Food we have to throw away doesn't count."

Guet Imm frowned. "Nobody likes a pedant, brother."

Her eyes flicked towards the pack on Tet Sang's back, containing the goods he was to deliver. She seemed to derive inspiration from it.

"It's because I'm a nun, isn't it?" she said. "You're scared my stomach is too delicate for your work. You don't have to worry. I understand what I signed up for."

Tet Sang shook his head. "You have an overblown idea of what we do."

Guet Imm looked unconvinced. "So, you're saying those"—she pointed at his pack—"are completely legal goods? Not even a little bit contraband?"

"What do you want with a group like us, anyway?" said Tet Sang, ignoring this. "There's a war on. Decent lady like you, you should be working in a shop or a house somewhere, with rice on the table and a bed to sleep in at night. Not on the road with some gangsters who've run out of options."

It was the first thing he'd said that had a real impact. Guet Imm's head whipped around, her mouth falling open. He'd begun to hope he'd got through to her when she said, "There's a *war* on?"

Tet Sang stared back, equally nonplussed. "You didn't *know*?"

"Of course not," sputtered Guet Imm. It was the most flustered he'd ever seen her. "Does everybody know? All the brothers?"

"Of course everybody knows, how do you not notice there's a war—" Tet Sang cut himself off. "Wait. How long were you in seclusion?"

"I went in when I was fifteen," said Guet Imm. "Roughly ten years ago."

"You came out when?"

The light went out of the nun's face. She said, "They burnt the tokong in the second month."

It was the fifth month now, so three months had

passed. Tet Sang did an internal calculation. The Reformist cause for which the bandits fought had begun to flower in the Tang motherland long before it travelled south to the peninsula. Reformism had become established among the Tang peoples in the Southern Seas only a decade or so ago. Local Reformists hadn't been considered bandits until after the Yamatese invasion that had put the Protector to flight. For a time, the Protectorate had even supported the Reformists' resistance against the Yamatese occupation, supplying the Reformists with weapons and military training.

It was only when the Protector retook the peninsula upon the withdrawal of the Yamatese army that the decisive breach had occurred. No longer in need of the Reformists to fight Yamato's soldiers, the Protectorate had outlawed the movement and begun its purges—jailing Reformist leaders and resettling populations under suspicion of sympathizing with Reformism.

Entire Tang villages were herded onto swampy, infertile land and subjected to armed surveillance, curfews, mass deportations. As for the monastic orders, they had always been centres for Tang education and community. The fact that the orders were prohibited by the rules of their religion from adopting any political affiliation made no difference to the Protector. He was not interested in what the votaries believed but in what they did, and it could not be denied that the orders fed, healed and sheltered

Reformists, as they were called upon to do for any ragged outcast who came to them. This was enough for the Protectorate: the Tang orders were being systematically burnt out of their tokong.

For all its efforts, the Protectorate had not yet succeeded in eliminating Reformism. The Reformists—bandits now—had gone into the jungle, where they were harder to purge, though the Protectorate was doing its best.

If Guet Imm had been in seclusion for a decade, shut off from news of the world, it perhaps explained why she had not known all this. Still . . .

"Didn't you find it weird when your tokong was burnt down?" said Tet Sang. "That's not the kind of thing that happens in a country at peace."

"It's not like I saw who did it," said Guet Imm, with uncharacteristic shrewishness. "There was nobody left to explain after I got out of my cell. Of course I knew there were problems. But even when I went to town and got a job, nobody talked about a war."

"Nobody talks about it. It's not that kind of war."

"What kind of war is it, then?" said Guet Imm. She looked like she wanted to hit Tet Sang. "A secret war? I've never heard of such a thing!"

"Yes," said Tet Sang. "Open death, open atrocity, open persecution. But a silent war. It's safer to be silent in these times."

Guet Imm bit her lip. For a while, neither spoke.

"How long has the country been at war?" she said finally.

"You mean this current war, or including the one before it also?"

"I don't know!" said Guet Imm. "I had no idea. I had no idea."

Tet Sang saw with an unpleasant shock that her eyes were full of tears. He raised his hand to pat her on the shoulder but thought better of it.

"The world changed while you were praying, sister," he said after a pause. It was the closest he could get to saying he was sorry.

———

Tet Sang was to meet his contact in the back room of a tailor's shop. He'd supposed the choice of location was because it was a front for illegal activities, but the real reason became clear when they approached the row of shophouses. The tailor occupied the lot at the very end, next to the river. Outside the entrance, trailing its branches in the water, was a willow tree.

"Religious people," muttered Tet Sang under his breath. It did not matter so long as the buyer paid up. But the sight of the tree had given him a nasty jolt.

Of course he was with the only member of the group who would recognise the symbol, even if she didn't know what it signified on this particular occasion.

Guet Imm said instantly, with delight, "The emblem

of the deity!" The Pure Moon was often depicted holding a willow branch, as a ward against evil. "Is that the shop we're going to, brother? That's a very good omen!"

"Why don't you go and find your herbalist?" said Tet Sang. It had been a couple of years since he had last been to Sungai Tombak, but it was a place to which change came slowly. "There should be one two streets over, if you turn left down there." He pointed.

Guet Imm looked hurt.

"I thought I was coming with you," she protested. "I could help with negotiations."

This might have worked on Ah Hin. Tet Sang was unmoved.

"I'm going straight back to camp when I'm finished," he said. "You want your rags, you better go get them now."

Guet Imm gave a dramatic sigh, but Tet Sang raised an eyebrow, waiting. After a moment, she spread her hands, smiling ruefully. "You can't blame me for trying, brother!"

"Watch the hem of your own sarong," Tet Sang told her, but he was perturbed to realise that he didn't in fact blame her. He found himself wanting to answer with a smile of his own.

The word *jampi* flitted through his mind—but that was the sort of witchcraft people who didn't know anything about the Order of the Pure Moon thought her followers indulged in. Tet Sang knew better.

He stood watching Guet Imm till she had turned off

the road and was lost to sight. Only once he was certain she was not coming back did he go into the tailor's shop. He was dissatisfied with himself, full of a vague unease.

Signs and portents; a sense of the world of seen things as shifting sands concealing a hidden core of marvels and terrors . . . he'd thought he'd left all of that behind long ago. But some forms of folly, like love and religion, were like lalang. Once established, they were almost impossible to eradicate.

The contact waiting in the dim back room of the tailor's shop brought Tet Sang down to earth. A bespectacled man with slick hair and the alert lidless eyes of a gecko, he seemed cleanly and decent, like a clerk. At the same time, there was something off-putting about him—one would not be surprised to hear that he embezzled funds or slapped his mother-in-law.

Tet Sang disliked him on sight, but there was something reassuring about him. Here was a person who belonged to Tet Sang's life as it was now.

"Mr Ng?" said Tet Sang. "I'm Lau's agent."

The contact gave him a disapproving once-over, not bothering to return Tet Sang's bow. "You have the objects?"

Tet Sang inclined his head. "You have the money?"

Ng's frown deepened. "I must examine the items first. Make sure they are authentic. Nowadays, there are a lot of fakes on the market, con men trying to pass off all kinds of rubbish."

"Not Lau Fung Cheung," said Tet Sang. He didn't so much as raise his voice, but Ng shut up. "Of course you will get to examine the goods before paying," he continued. "But I want to see the money first. You haven't shown any proof of who you're acting for."

Ng flushed, but he glanced back at the shop, where the tailor and his sons were at work. Mr Tan and his sons were each six feet tall and half again as wide, and their custom came entirely from the town's rich families, who were connected with the Tang wealthy all over the peninsula—a golden network, exerting significant influence even in these troubled times.

The thought of the tailor's dependency on his boss no doubt comforted Ng. He reached into his robes, producing a handful of cash.

"The rest is in a chest in front there," he said, jerking his head at the shop. "Mr Tan is looking after it for me."

"The balance, as agreed?" said Tet Sang. They had already been paid half the purchase price as a deposit.

"You can count the money when I've examined the goods," said Ng.

Tet Sang nodded. He put his pack on the table between them and lifted out the goods one by one. They were wrapped in cloth, so he did not need to touch them directly. But though it was through him that Fung Cheung had got the goods, Tet Sang had had nothing more to do with them since, except to carry the pack. He was not prepared for the faint scent of incense that rose from the bundles.

It was like being punched in the gut. He froze, bent over and gasping. While he breathed through the shock, Ng reached out, a covetous light in his eye.

Ng pulled back the cloth on a bundle, revealing a gold chalice carved in the form of a lotus. It was exquisite—the product of years of painstaking work by craftswomen of the highest order—but the real treasure was tucked in the heart of the lotus, cradled by its petals.

"Ah!" breathed Ng. Recollecting himself, he assumed an unimpressed air. "You have proof that's real gold?"

Tet Sang gave him an incredulous look. Before he could answer, a screech like the battle cry of a cat made them jump. A grey-robed wind swept through the room, seizing the chalice.

"Oi!" shouted Ng.

Guet Imm ignored him. She was staring at Tet Sang, her eyes like holes burnt in parchment.

"What are you doing?" she said. "This is a sacred relic of the deity!"

"Who the fuck are you?" said Ng. He turned to Tet Sang. "Who the fuck is this? Do you know her?"

Tet Sang should have known this would happen. He thought of the willow tree at the shop entrance.

But he couldn't blame the deity. The decision to let Guet Imm come along had been all his own.

"She's a nun, obviously," he said. "I told you the goods were authentic."

"How dare you try to sell the deity's sarira?" said Guet Imm to Tet Sang. Ng might have been invisible for all the attention she paid him. "It's beyond value! Where did you even get it?"

"Where do you usually get relics?" said Tet Sang.

"What do you think you're doing?" said Ng sharply.

Guet Imm was scrabbling through the bundles, tearing off the cloth. An embarrassment of riches spilt out onto the table—jade prayer beads, engraved gold plate, a prayer wheel studded with jewels, an exquisite porcelain statue of the Pure Moon. The nun made a huffy yowl of outrage at each treasure that emerged.

"You looted a tokong," she snarled at Tet Sang. "You—you *blasphemer*! The deity should strike you down!"

"Take your hands off those things," said Ng. "They belong to my boss!"

He strode over to the table, snatching up the prayer beads, but he couldn't manage to get anything else. Guet Imm was busy rewrapping the statue in cloth but somehow managed to keep it and the other artefacts out of Ng's reach without any apparent effort. Turning red, Ng raised his hand.

Guet Imm was being annoying, and the word *blasphemer* had stung Tet Sang out of all proportion to its proper force. But if there was going to be a fight, he would prefer that she was not involved. He caught Ng's hand before the man could do anything foolish with it.

"You're being a little premature, Mr Ng," said Tet Sang. "You never paid yet also."

Ng glared at him, pop-eyed. "You—! Do you want this eight hundred cash or not?"

"You're selling these things for eight hundred cash?" said Guet Imm, raising her head. "That's ridiculous!"

"Listen to the nun!" said Ng. "My boss is no fool. If I tell him you're trying to cheat him, you can forget about the money. You want this deal, you better watch yourself."

"The statue alone is worth more than that," said Guet Imm, ignoring him. "With everything else, you should be asking for five taels of silver minimum.

"Not including the relic," she added. "You shouldn't even be thinking of selling the relic. Do you *want* to be cursed by the deity?"

Ng's face darkened. He said to Tet Sang, "If you don't get rid of this girl, I will."

Tet Sang raised his hands. "Let's not be hasty, Mr Ng—"

"Oh, yes," said Guet Imm, giving Ng a scalding look of contempt. "If you're going to outrage the relics of the deity's own precious body, why not her followers as well? You know, it's a misconception that you can only go to hell once."

"Shut up!" said Tet Sang. "You are not helping!"

At this juncture, one of the tailor's large sons burst in, wild-eyed.

"Mr Ng, the mata are outside," he said. "You better go, sir!"

Ng's head swivelled towards Tet Sang and Guet Imm. If looks could kill, they would have been descending rapidly through the ten hells at that very moment.

"You," Ng sputtered. "You set us up!"

Tet Sang was baffled. "You think *we're* friends of the mata?"

"My boss will hear of this," said Ng. "You can rest assured I'll tell him you're not real bandits!"

"We never said we were bandits," said Tet Sang, exasperated. "Who ever heard of bandits having valuables to sell? They live in the jungle!"

"Sir!" said the tailor's son urgently. He pushed open what turned out to be a grille door, which had previously been obscured by rolls of cloth.

Ng cast a last glower at Tet Sang before vanishing out of the door.

"Come back!" shouted Guet Imm. She turned to Tet Sang, her face alight with indignation. "He took the prayer beads!"

"Never mind," said Tet Sang. "Let's get out of here."

But they'd left it too late, and all the yelling hadn't helped. They heard the tramp of heavy feet. The tailor's son had just enough time to wrench the back door shut and put himself in front of it before the mata came in.

There were three of them, much smaller than the tailor

and his sons, but they carried guns. Two were Malayu, like most of the mata; the third was Damilan. The tailor's wife, Madam Ooi, accompanied them.

"You said this was a storeroom," said one of the mata to her in the common tongue—evidently the chief. The other two mata hung back behind him.

"It's a storeroom what," said Madam Ooi belligerently. "See all that batik!" She gestured at the rolls of cloth on the floor.

The mata was looking at the table, with the tokong goods spread out in all their glory. "I didn't know tailors stored such things."

He put out his rifle, nudging the statue. It rolled over, the Pure Moon's face serene despite the indignity of her position.

Guet Imm made an aborted movement, but Tet Sang grabbed her arm, pulling her back. The mata raised his head, looking directly at Tet Sang.

"And here is the bandit Lau Fung Cheung," said the mata. He clicked his tongue. "Can you tell me why you have a wanted criminal in your storeroom, madam?"

"Must be he broke in," said Madam Ooi, with admirable composure. "Aiyah, so many times I told my husband to fix the back-door lock, but he never listened! Boy, this stranger didn't hurt you, did he?"

Her son clearly hadn't inherited Madam Ooi's wits. He looked confused. "What?"

"How do you know Lau Fung Cheung?" said the mata to the tailor's wife.

It was natural that he should have mistaken Tet Sang for Fung Cheung, given that the pictures on the Protectorate's wanted poster had been no sort of likeness. Still, it was a little surprising—Lau Fung Cheung had a reputation for beauty. Perhaps Tet Sang should feel flattered.

"She doesn't," he said. "I never told Mr Tan and Madam Ooi my name." Strictly, this was true. "Who told you Lau Fung Cheung was here?"

"We followed your tracks based on a report from a worthy citizen," said the mata. "You shouldn't pick fights in people's coffeehouses, Mr Lau."

"Mr Aw!" gasped Guet Imm. "Who knew he was so ungrateful? After you gave him all that money!"

"I'll be more careful next time," said Tet Sang, ignoring her, but the mata grinned.

"Boss," he said, "there won't be a next time. You know what the punishment for banditry is."

Tet Sang did. He'd seen the posters—triumphant men in uniform, brandishing severed heads. The Protectorate wanted the Reformists to understand what it had in store for them.

"What's the going rate these days?" said Tet Sang. "Twenty cash per head? I can give you more if you let us go quietly. We don't want trouble."

He said it more as a good-faith effort to avoid a bust-up

than because he thought the offer would be accepted. It might have worked if there had only been one mata, but the chief wasn't likely to take a bribe in front of his subordinates.

"I don't negotiate with bandits," he sneered. He raised his gun.

Tet Sang dodged before the mata could bring the gun down on his head, landing heavily on the floor. But Guet Imm was faster. She flipped the table, knocking over all three men. The gun went off, the report deafening in the small room.

The tailor's wife screamed, but the bullet couldn't have gone anywhere near her. Guet Imm nodded when Tet Sang glanced at her, to show she was fine.

"Open the door, little brother," Tet Sang said to the tailor's son.

The youth hesitated.

"Pukimak!" groaned one of the mata on the floor. He started struggling to his feet. Guet Imm threw the chalice at his head, dropping him.

The other two stayed down, but that didn't necessarily mean they were unconscious. Tet Sang saw the tailor's son's difficulty.

"Let us out or we'll hurt you," Tet Sang said loudly.

"You'd better hurt him anyway, or the mata won't believe," screamed Madam Ooi in Tang dialect. "No need to draw blood. It'll be enough to bruise him a little. Boy, don't fight back!"

"But Ma!" said her son, quailing.

Guet Imm moved so quickly, Tet Sang didn't see what she did, but the youth's protest ended in a pained yelp. The tailor's son staggered forward, holding his head and falling against the door as though by accident. The door swung open.

Tet Sang charged forward, pretending to shove the youth out of the way, and he and Guet Imm were out, running down the alley behind the shophouses. Madam Ooi's voice drifted through the open door behind them:

"Tuan, tuan, help my son! Those cruel bandits hurt him! Oh, boy, boy!"

"Helpful woman," muttered Tet Sang. Fung Cheung had remarked that Mr Tan was an old associate, but Tet Sang wondered whether the connection wasn't really with the wife. Women went soft around Fung Cheung—not only his beauty but his feyness seemed to turn their heads. "What did you do to that boy?"

"Nothing serious," said Guet Imm. "It'll look worse than it is." Without warning, she thumped him on the side of his head.

Tet Sang swore, his hand flying to his head. "What the hell?"

"No wonder you wouldn't tell me what you were selling!" said Guet Imm. "How could you? Hawking off the deity's sarira as though they're—they're—" They rounded a corner, passing a rattan shop with its wares spilling out onto the five-foot way. "As though they're nothing more than baskets!"

"Wait," said Tet Sang.

Two doors down from the rattan shop was one of the many abandoned shoplots that could be found in Sungai Tombak, despite its relative prosperity—people's livelihoods were one of the many casualties of the ongoing struggle between the Protectorate and the bandits. Tet Sang pushed past a rusting grille into a shadowy doorway, dragging Guet Imm in after him.

Guet Imm hadn't stopped talking. "You know or not how many tokong they destroyed? How many people died trying to protect the altars?"

"At the Pure Moon tokong at Permatang Timbul, it was thirty-nine," said Tet Sang. He shoved a batik cloth he'd grabbed on the way out of the tailor's shop at Guet Imm. "Take off your robes. You know how to wear a sarong?"

"They— What?"

"If you don't know how to tie, I can show you," said Tet Sang.

"No, I know how to wear a sarong, I—What did you say about the tokong?"

"Thirty-nine died," said Tet Sang. "They didn't die protecting the altars. Most of them ran. Just not fast enough."

Guet Imm stared.

"Brother," she said helplessly.

Tet Sang saw that he would have difficulty getting her

to focus. He shouldn't have answered her question. He'd spoken in part to distract himself from his own discomfort; of course he would not look, but it was awkward asking Guet Imm to disrobe in front of him.

But there were more important things to worry about than awkwardness. The mata were taking longer to come after them than he'd expected—thanks, probably, to the tailor's wife—but the sooner they were out of Sungai Tombak, the better.

"Put on your sarong," he said. "We have to get to the main road and get out of town. Right now, people will be going to market. We need to blend in. There'll be plenty of men looking like me. Men escorting a nun, not so much."

He looked at Guet Imm's head, frowning. It had sprouted a thin fuzz since she'd joined the group, but it would still single her out in the market-going crowd. Then he had an inspiration.

"You stay here and change," he said. "I'll be back."

He wasn't gone for long. Guet Imm was knotting her sarong by the time he returned. She might have worn a sarong before, but her fumbling hands suggested it hadn't been often. It wasn't likely her ikat would hold.

"Let me do," said Tet Sang.

He retied the cloth, focusing on the print. It was a colourful patterned import from the islands south of the peninsula, of the kind popular among Tang matrons. The style was a little old for Guet Imm, but it wasn't like he'd had the luxury to pick and choose.

He'd never seen Guet Imm's shoulders before. She smelt of sweat, but there was no trace of the scent of fear. Tet Sang would have recognised it.

He tried to touch her as little as possible.

When he was done, he set on her head what he'd picked up from the rattan shop—a wide-brimmed farmer's hat, casting all beneath it into shade. It looked a little strange—farmers didn't go around in sarongs with their arms exposed to the elements—but it would stand out less than Guet Imm's bare head. He put another hat on his own head and shoved Guet Imm's votarial robes into a rattan basket.

"Did you pay for these?" said Guet Imm, touching her hat.

"If you sleep in your shop," said Tet Sang, "you can't complain when people steal your wares."

In fact, he had left some coins as payment. But he'd already betrayed too much about himself to Guet Imm that day.

"Let's go," he said.

五

"Eight hundred cash down the drain," said Fung Cheung. "Eight hundred cash!" He ran his hands through his hair.

Tet Sang sat erect with his hands on his knees, trying to ignore the pounding at his temples. It had been a long, hot march from the sundry shop, where they had picked up Rimau and Ah Boon, to their camp. As if baking in the blistering midday sun wasn't enough, now he had to deal with Fung Cheung throwing a tantrum while the others packed up around them.

Guet Imm was uncharacteristically quiet. He found himself wishing for once that she would talk—cajole Fung Cheung out of his foul mood with her quicksilver charm. Lacking charm, Tet Sang fell back on common sense.

"Ng's boss won't want to make trouble," he said. "He's close to the Protector. Any rumour he's working with people like us would cause problems for him. If he's smart, he'll leave us alone. He risks more by chasing us."

"Not if he tells the Protectorate we stole one thousand six hundred cash from him," said Fung Cheung.

Tet Sang's head was swimming. It was hard to focus on what Fung Cheung was saying. It took a moment before he understood.

"You mean the deposit," said Tet Sang. "But that was only eight hundred cash."

"And where do you think the balance went?" said Fung Cheung witheringly. "You think this Mr Ng took the chest with the rest of the money back to his boss? Even if he split with Mr Tan to keep him quiet, that's four hundred each. All he has to do is tell his boss we ran away with it."

Tet Sang's headache was getting worse.

"Okay," he said. "Maybe you're right. But the buyer is a fair man. If we go to him directly and explain, he'll understand. He of all people should know there was always a risk of interference from the mata. Even if we can only pay back half, that's better than nothing. There's no reason for us to give back the deposit if we were really trying to steal from him."

"That's not an option," said Fung Cheung.

Tet Sang stared, but Fung Cheung wouldn't meet his eyes. A sickening certainty descended on him.

"We said we would keep the money until the job was done," said Tet Sang.

"We had to pay for the rice. Nobody gives credit for rice these days."

"You didn't spend eight hundred cash on *rice*. We were going to use the takings from the last job. What happened to that?"

Tet Sang would have been more tactful if he'd been less tired. In a good mood, Fung Cheung took scoldings well, but with the loss of face from this embarrassing revelation, being shamed could only make him angrier. Sure enough, he snapped:

"It wouldn't matter if your nun didn't fuck up the deal!"

"*My* nun? I told you not to take her on in the first place!"

"Who was the one who took her to town?" Fung Cheung retorted.

"You all sound like a married couple," observed Guet Imm. Incredibly, she sounded amused.

This was not the kind of intervention Tet Sang had been hoping for. He and Fung Cheung both turned to glare at her.

"And you!" said Fung Cheung. "Who asked you to interfere in the deal?"

Guet Imm seemed genuinely mystified. "I'm a follower of the Pure Moon, brother. If I find out you're selling the deity's relics, of course I must interfere. Lucky I was there," she added. "If the sale went through, who knows what would have happened? The deity is merciful, but she is like any god. You cannot cross the line."

"Better to let the tokong goods burn, is it?" said Fung Cheung. "Or maybe the deity would prefer it if the Protector takes them and puts them in a museum in his country for unbelievers to look at? That's his usual tactic. Maybe we can't all chant sutras, but you're not the only one who knows how to respect the gods. We didn't simply decide to sell the goods to anybody. Yeoh Thean Tee would have looked after them properly."

Guet Imm's expression flickered. "Yeoh Thean Tee?"

"Even nuns have heard of him, hah?" said Fung Cheung.

He was not being serious. Yeoh Thean Tee was the head of one of the wealthiest families on the peninsula—and at one point, the Southern Seas' most generous donor to the monastic orders. It would have been unheard of for even the most secluded anchorite not to recognise the Yeoh name.

"The Yeoh family paid for our turtle pond," said Guet Imm. "Yeoh Thean Tee's daughter was an acolyte of the Order."

She seemed dumbfounded. After a moment, she said,

"But he doesn't live in Sungai Tombak, does he? I thought he was based in the capital."

Tet Sang snorted. "You think Yeoh Thean Tee meets the butcher who supplies his siew yoke? We only talked to his agents."

"You cannot make money if you offend the Protector," said Fung Cheung. "But the Yeoh family has always supported the religious orders. They cannot say anything openly, but they don't like what is happening to the tokong. They want to save the tokong goods for future generations."

"Forget about saving the current generation," said Tet Sang. "They are merely human beings. Not valuable."

Fung Cheung rolled his eyes. They'd had this argument before.

"It's not like you could put people in a sack and smuggle them out without the mata noticing," he said. "Isn't it better if the goods are saved at least?"

"So, they asked you to—what? Steal treasures from the tokong before the mata could get to them?" said Guet Imm.

"After," said Tet Sang. "They asked for any sacred artefacts left in the tokong after the mata came."

"And just so happen you had some sacred artefacts lying around?" said Guet Imm sceptically.

Fortunately, she was looking at Fung Cheung. His expression did not change.

"Just so happen we had some," he agreed. "Lucky, right?"

Guet Imm gave him a look of suspicion. She opened her mouth.

"When Fate decides, it's not for us to quarrel," said Tet Sang. "It wasn't humans who sent the Yeohs to us."

He hadn't planned to speak, and he heard his own words with surprise. To his disgust, he found he believed what he said, though until then, he would have said that he no longer followed any gods nor put much credence in their powers. He would have preferred to have been spared this self-knowledge.

Guet Imm looked equally surprised, but after a moment, she recovered her customary sangfroid.

"Maybe the Yeoh family is pious, but they were cheating you," she said. "The statue was very good quality— handmade by northern craftsmen. You could have earned a tael from that alone."

"Good thing we don't have it anymore, then," said Fung Cheung drily. "At least we won't be cheated. Instead, we're in trouble with the most powerful Tang family in the country. The Protector went to Yeoh Thean Tee's eldest son's wedding."

A polite cough interrupted him.

"Cheung," said Rimau. "We're done."

He jerked his head at the rest of the group. The brothers stood ready to leave with all they had strapped to their backs, trying to look as though they hadn't been listening in on the entire conversation.

Fung Cheung held Guet Imm's eyes for a moment.

"Fine," he said. "Let's go." He rose, breaking the gaze.

Rimau was a courteous soul and it was obvious it pained him to ask, but he said in a low voice, "What about her?" His eyes flicked towards Guet Imm.

Tet Sang thought of the chalice—the one true treasure among the tokong goods they'd brought to Sungai Tombak. The other artefacts had merely been valuable. The chalice—and what it held—were irreplaceable. Guet Imm had thrown it at the mata without hesitation.

"She comes with us," he said.

Rimau looked at Fung Cheung.

Tet Sang was prepared to defend Guet Imm—explain that it was not her fault the mata had been put onto them; that she'd helped fend the mata off, even if he was reasonably sure he could've got out of the tailor's shop without her help. But angry as Fung Cheung was, Tet Sang knew he wouldn't have to argue.

He was right.

"You heard Ah Sang," said Fung Cheung. "Let's go."

"Where are we going?" said Guet Imm, in a subdued voice.

Fung Cheung didn't respond at once. Tet Sang saw that he didn't know the answer.

They'd had plans for what they were going to do once

they completed the job and had one thousand six hundred cash at their disposal. They hadn't planned for the job going wrong.

It was usually Tet Sang who made sure there was a backup plan. He hadn't done it this time, because—he realised now—in his inmost heart, he had believed it was Heaven's design that this deal should happen. He had been convinced that they were meant to entrust what remained of the tokong at Permatang Timbul to some of the few people on the peninsula who knew the value of the treasures and had a hope of surviving the current turmoil.

"We're going to get lost," said Fung Cheung finally.

There was a trail running parallel to the waterfall by which they had camped. It went up the slope before plunging into parts unknown, deep in the jungle. Fung Cheung looked at it without pleasure.

"It's a good thing you know how to deal with leeches, Sister Guet Imm," he said. "We're going to need it."

———

Fung Cheung wanted to go as far into the jungle as they could before darkness fell. The deeper they were, the safer they would be from the mata. The wilderness held other terrors, of course, but for now they faded into insignificance beside the concrete threat of the Protectorate.

It was not till nighttime that they stopped and pitched camp. Tet Sang hadn't been sure how he would summon the energy to put up his shelter, but Rimau—who was somewhat more insightful than the others—stepped in to help. Tet Sang was too weary to protest.

At least Rimau had tact. Once the shelter was up, he did not trouble Tet Sang with questions or solicitude, but clapped him on the shoulder and went off.

Peace and quiet, thought Tet Sang. He felt like a man in a desert lifting a gourd of water to his lips.

He had started taking off his clothes when Guet Imm said into his ear: "There were only twenty-one votaries at Permatang Timbul."

"Argh!" said Tet Sang. He pulled his underrobe back on hastily.

As usual, his shelter was some distance from the others'. He should have seen Guet Imm coming. But there had been no sign of her approach—just empty air all around, before she'd popped into existence like a ghost.

"Don't do that!" he snapped. "I almost punched you."

He expected an airy dismissal, but the nun was staring. She caught the hem of Tet Sang's underrobe and drew it up, revealing the bandage.

"You're hurt," she said. "When . . ."

"It's nothing," said Tet Sang, shaking Guet Imm off.

She dropped her hand, but she'd worked out the answer for herself. "The mata's gun that went off."

Tet Sang had barely noticed the bullet at the time.

He'd felt the red heat scoring his side, but it had seemed distant, unimportant, given everything else going on.

It had started to hurt worse while they were getting out of Sungai Tombak, but it was still ignorable. His layers of robes meant that the stain wasn't obvious even as it spread.

It had been the march into the forest that had been the worst trial. He'd managed to change his clothes and dress the wound before they set off into the jungle, but rest had been out of the question. As Tet Sang had stumbled through the undergrowth, dizzy and sick, the journey had taken on a nightmare quality.

Guet Imm's fists were clenched. So much for peace and quiet.

"You didn't say anything!" she said accusingly.

"It's just a graze," said Tet Sang.

Without quite knowing how it happened, he found himself sitting down. Guet Imm got his makeshift bandage off, her deft hands light against his skin. Her forehead smoothed out as she inspected the wound, but she still looked annoyed.

"No wonder you looked so bad," she murmured. "I thought you were angry."

"I washed the wound," said Tet Sang. "There's nothing more to do."

He might as well have stayed silent for all the notice Guet Imm took of him.

"I can make herbal soup for you. It'll help the healing,"

she said. "I'll call Ah Boon to dress the wound. He has some medicine."

She got up, but Tet Sang grabbed her. "No!"

Guet Imm paused, looking down at him. Her face was in shadow, so he couldn't see her expression. She said, with uncharacteristic hesitancy, "You don't want him to know?"

"Fuss, fuss, fuss," said Tet Sang irritably. "Ah Lau is like an old woman about this kind of thing. He'll act like I'm halfway dead. What's the point of making a big hoo-ha? It's stopped bleeding already."

It was only when Guet Imm did not answer that he realised she had not been talking about the injury.

She dropped into a squat, looking into his eyes as though she could see through to the back of his head.

Panic bubbled inside him. She knew. Perhaps she'd known all along. He'd taken pains to hide it, but he should've tried harder. And if she hadn't already known, she would've realised when he talked about Permatang Timbul. Idiot that he was . . .

"Brother," said Guet Imm. "Does everyone know you're a woman?"

Tet Sang blinked.

"Ah Lau, yes," he said. "The rest, maybe. We haven't talked about it. Why?"

"I didn't realise at first," said Guet Imm. "Why didn't you tell me?"

"You didn't ask also." Hope flickered to life within Tet

Sang. If this was all it was . . . ! He said cautiously, "What made you realise?"

"When you knew about kacip fatimah, I should have wondered," said Guet Imm. "But it was when you tied my sarong. You really knew how to do it. The ikat didn't budge. If I did it myself, I would have lost the sarong by the time we were on the main street."

She rose.

"If you don't want Ah Boon to see it," she said, "let me put the dressing, then."

Tet Sang reached out to detain her. "There's no need . . ."

But Guet Imm had already left.

———

Tet Sang got his peace and quiet after all. Guet Imm came back with supplies and set to work without saying anything, cleaning and re-dressing the wound in blessed silence.

Her work was certainly neater than Tet Sang's had been. It was a task well within his abilities, but he hadn't been at his best when he'd first bandaged himself up, and it had had to be done quickly.

He started to relax despite himself. There was something soothing in Guet Imm's closeness. She smelt right. He tried not to think about what that meant.

At least the injury was distracting her. She hadn't asked about Permatang Timbul again. Maybe she wouldn't ask. He'd rather be interrogated about what lay beneath his robes.

Tet Sang had never discussed the matter with Fung Cheung in so many words, not even to ask him to refrain from telling the others. After all, it was Fung Cheung's group. It was for him to decide what the men should know.

But there had never been any sign that Fung Cheung had told. As for Tet Sang, it came naturally to say nothing about himself, to remain slightly apart from the rest of the group. It was less that he minded the brothers knowing what he was than that he feared what that might lead to—other questions, about *who* he was. Those he had no wish to answer.

Guet Imm was being more respectful than the men would probably have been, but then, people like Tet Sang were not unheard-of in the monastic orders. Attitudes varied, but the Pure Moon was a fairly relaxed deity in this regard. Though it was controversial in certain tokong to say so, she had historically been worshipped in male incarnations; even now, there were countries where the deity was chiefly known as a male god. As the Pure Moon, she only accepted women as her votaries, but her doctrine allowed her followers to decide for themselves whether they were women enough to count.

Tet Sang had known of members of her Order who had been dedicated to the Pure Moon at a young age but then decided they could not endure to be called *sister*. They had departed to join male orders or start other lives. Conversely, he had no doubt that some of the Pure Moon's nuns had lived as men before they joined her Order. Once they entered the deity's light, no one was particularly interested in what they had been before.

"We should have taken you on as a healer," said Tet Sang, by way of saying thank you. "You're better at this than cooking."

The ends of Guet Imm's mouth turned up, but it wasn't much like a smile. "Better not to hurt Ah Boon's feelings. He's good at what he does. It's just cows are not that similar to humans."

She was evidently preoccupied, however. In a moment, it came out.

"I wondered about Brother Lau," she said. "Sometimes, the way he looks at you . . ."

Tet Sang waited, but no follow-up came. "How does he look at me?"

"Like he's in love with you," said Guet Imm.

Tet Sang gaped.

Guet Imm's ears were pink. He hadn't known she was capable of blushing.

"You're not interested?" she said, with a feeble pretence of nonchalance. "He's very good-looking."

Tet Sang snorted, reassured. "His one virtue."

So, that was what this was about. Their nun had conceived a passion for Fung Cheung. It was a bad lookout for her, but she was not the first woman it had happened to and she would not be the last.

"You know Ah Lau likes men," he said, not unkindly. "He won't say no to a woman, but he is not serious about them."

Guet Imm couldn't seem to decide whether she wanted to look at Tet Sang or not. She kept glancing at him, but whenever their eyes met, her gaze skittered away.

"He's serious about you," she said. "Everyone pretends Brother Lau is the boss, but you're the one he listens to."

"You're seeing things that are not there, sister," said Tet Sang, amused.

Guet Imm raised an eyebrow. "I'm a nun. Seeing things that aren't there is my speciality. You're telling me he's never asked?"

To his annoyance, Tet Sang felt warmth rise in his face. "When Ah Lau is bored, a piece of wood also he'll ask. It doesn't mean anything. Why do you care?"

If he'd been hoping to discomfit her, he was disappointed. Guet Imm tossed her head.

"I'm surprised, that's all," she said. "Not many people—man or woman—would say no to Brother Lau."

"Unlike many people," said Tet Sang, "I *know* Ah Lau."

Guet Imm still wasn't convinced.

"But what if it did mean something, when he asked?" she persisted. "What if I'm right?"

Tet Sang had told Guet Imm the truth—he'd never been interested in Fung Cheung in that way. Even if his inclinations had lain in that direction, his intimate familiarity with Fung Cheung's personality would have put him off. But if Guet Imm liked Fung Cheung, perhaps it would make her feel better to believe she was not alone.

"What's the point of talking about 'what if'?" he said, in a tone to make it clear he'd said all he would on the topic.

Guet Imm could take that for confirmation of his interest in Fung Cheung if she liked. She would not be the first to suspect Tet Sang of harbouring feelings for Fung Cheung going beyond pure brotherhood.

Guet Imm finished her work, letting Tet Sang's underrobe fall over the new dressing. "It should be changed every few hours. Call me and I'll do for you."

She paused, slanting a tentative look at him.

"So, you *are* a woman?" she said. "The scriptures say there are souls who lose their way after they die. They go into the wrong body by accident when they are reborn. There was a nun at my tokong like that. She was a son to her parents before she decided to follow the deity."

Guet Imm would accept whatever answer Tet Sang gave her. Yet he hesitated. He put on his outer robes without speaking and went to the edge of the shelter, looking out at the forest.

He hadn't thought too hard about the new identity he had assumed—a long time before now, it felt. Putting on men's clothes, a man's name, had been a practical choice amid the chaos of the war. It wasn't like there had been anything left of what had gone before. There had been no one to consult, to challenge, to remember the person Tet Sang had been before the breach.

He'd never had to consider the questions that came to him now. The words were strange on his tongue as he spoke.

"What does it mean to be a woman or a man?" he said. "I live the life of a man, but my heart hasn't changed from when I was a woman. This"—he gestured at himself—"is the body of a woman. But it carries the sins of a man."

"Women can be sinful too, you know," said Guet Imm.

Tet Sang smiled without amusement. "Oh, yes? What do *you* know of sin, sister?"

"It's true, what do I know?" said Guet Imm sadly. "I never had a chance to find out. I went into seclusion too young. I was not clever like you, brother. It never occurred to me to look beyond the Order."

It was like Tet Sang had been walking on a sunlit path until Guet Imm said these last words and plunged him into shadow. Chilled, he said, "What do you mean?"

Guet Imm was sitting on the ground, legs crossed. It was a position Tet Sang knew in his very bones. One could hold it through hours of meditation.

"You always questioned the Order, I think," she said. "Even before you left your tokong."

Tet Sang froze.

"You were a follower of the Pure Moon, weren't you?" said Guet Imm. "There were only twenty-one votaries at Permatang Timbul. That, a layperson might know. But the others . . ."

There hadn't just been nuns at the tokong of the Pure Moon at Permatang Timbul. They had had their full complement of cooks and cleaners and labourers, who looked after the votaries; orphans and the indigent and the elderly, whom the votaries looked after in their turn.

"You would only know how many died if you were there," said Guet Imm.

There was a roaring in Tet Sang's ears. Stupid, *stupid* to lower his guard. What had he thought? That she'd simply forget what he'd let slip?

"You didn't have to be a nun to hear about the purges," he said through the roaring. "The Protectorate razed the tokong to the ground. The news was all over town."

Guet Imm blinked. "The mata did it? It was bandits who came to my tokong."

"There are enemies on both sides of the war," said Tet Sang. Then he realised the implications of what she'd said. "Wait. If the bandits destroyed your tokong, why did you join us? You thought *we* were bandits."

"I lost my job and you came to me, all in one day," said Guet Imm. "Obviously, the deity sent you to me. One way or another, I had to follow you.

"At first, I thought she wanted me to take revenge," she

added. "I bought a knife with the money you gave me, so I could do it while you were sleeping. I could have used poison—that would have been cleaner—but I wasn't sure I could find the right herbs in time."

"You came so you could kill us?" said Tet Sang. "After I gave you money?"

Guet Imm flapped a dismissive hand. "What is money?"

"Spoken like an anchorite," said Tet Sang. "Of course money has no meaning, when you've been living off people's donations all your life!"

"I don't know why you're so angry," said Guet Imm pettishly. "It's not like I was going to do it without a sign from the deity. In the end, I realised that was not her intention."

"What was her intention?"

Guet Imm did not answer this directly.

"I only became certain of who you were when you tied my sarong," she said.

Tet Sang frowned. "A nun wouldn't know how to tie a sarong. Look at you."

"No," said Guet Imm agreeably. "You must have learnt before you entered the Order. But when you did it, I saw your pendant."

Tet Sang's hand went to his chest, touching the small lump under his robes—the jade pendant he wore next to his skin, carved in the shape of the Pure Moon making the gesture of teaching. Anyone could wear a Pure Moon pendant, and often did, the deity being especially popular among the poor, the sick and women, but the pendants sold to laypeople invariably displayed her in the posture signifying compassion. It was her votaries who wore the image of the Pure Moon in the act of transmitting her wisdom.

"The deity must have been getting impatient," Guet Imm was saying. "It was very slow of me! I should have realised earlier you used to be a sister."

"You're talking nonsense," said Tet Sang. "Do I look like a religious?" He'd let his hair grow out; his face was brown and leathery from the sun. Certainly, no one looking at him would suspect him of ever having had a shaven head or worn grey votarial robes. The pendant he could have stolen, after all.

"No," said Guet Imm. "You look like a disreputable bandit who should cut his hair. But it's not your looks. You're moonlight on the water, brother. I should have known what you were from the start."

Tet Sang had meant to keep denying it, but the compliment took him off guard. There was no higher praise a devotee of the Pure Moon could give than to say of a person that they reflected the light of the deity. The last time he had received the commendation, it had been from the Abbot at Permatang Timbul.

The memory was sudden and extraordinarily vivid— the Abbot's elusive smile; her watery eyes, magnified by spectacles; Tet Sang's surprise and pleasure. The particular smell of the tokong rose in his nostrils, made up of the mingled scents of sandalwood smoke, burnt paper, food cooking in the kitchens and green growing things. For they had had gardens, grown their own vegetables and fruit. Everyone had worked in them, votaries and lay-people alike . . .

It was like being stabbed. Tet Sang barely noticed the sting of Guet Imm's follow-up: "At least, I *thought* you were good," she was saying. "At that time, I didn't know you were selling off the deity's relics to the highest bidder."

"You want to know what happened at Permatang Timbul, why the mata came after us?" said Tet Sang abruptly. "I'll tell you. They found out the Abbot was helping bandits. She would have done the same for the mata if they came to her sick and hungry," he added. "But that didn't matter. And that wasn't all. The Protectorate suspected the bandits were using the tokong as a meeting place. They thought there was some kind of conspiracy afoot."

"Was there?" said Guet Imm.

Tet Sang shrugged. The insinuation against the Abbot could not offend. He was already full up on anger, with no space left for more. "Who knows? The bandits had their own agenda. But the Abbot wouldn't have colluded. She was very orthodox. She didn't believe in getting involved in politics."

Despite his fury, Guet Imm's stillness was calming.

There were no pointless exclamations of surprise or sympathy to fend off.

"Your Abbot was one of the thirty-nine?" she said.

"There was no warning," said Tet Sang. "The mata came in the afternoon, when everyone was praying. The Abbot was resting; she was almost ninety. They ransacked the Abbot's office and took her out into the courtyard. Not that they meant to kill her. They wanted to interrogate her, but"—a smile twisted his lips—"she fought. One of the young fellows panicked and shot her.

"It was not the worst tragedy that day," he added. This was what he had told himself time and again, reminding himself to be measured in his grief. "She had a long life already. Most of the people who died were younger, not votaries. They were the people who helped in the kitchens, the gardens, the poor people the tokong took in. . . . Half the religious were away, visiting another tokong."

"Including you?"

Tet Sang shook his head. "I was there when it happened."

He'd gone to the Abbot when the mata left her for dead, but she hadn't actually died in his arms. She had made him promise he would look after the tokong's treasures, so he had had to leave her.

He had wondered, later, if it had been the survival of the treasures that had really concerned her. She had always been a thoroughly human Abbot, more concerned with souls than things. If not for the promise he'd made her, he would not have hidden in the narrow space behind the main altar. He would not have stayed put, cramped and sweating, as the sounds of the slaughter came to him. When finally the screams had stopped and he'd smelt smoke, heard the roar of the fires the mata had set, he might have decided to allow the flames to consume him, as they would consume the only home he had known.

Instead, he had thought of the treasures and run.

"I don't think the mata intended to destroy the tokong," said Tet Sang. "That was in the early days, before the Protectorate really started targeting the orders. But the raid went wrong. The mata had to cover up their uselessness. Later, they put out some story about finding bandits hiding in the tokong, said there was a big fight and the bandits set fire to the place so they could get away. The Protectorate posted notices in town, warning people. They said, *That's what happens when you help bandits.*"

"What happened to the other votaries? The ones who weren't there."

Tet Sang shrugged. "The smart ones disappeared. The ones who went to the Protectorate when they came back and found the tokong destroyed got resettled. One or two got executed for conspiring with bandits."

Guet Imm did not ask if they had been guilty. She must have known that that was of no importance.

"The bandits thought we were conspiring with the

mata at my tokong," she said. "They thought we were spying on them and reporting back to the Protectorate. That's why they came after us—at least, I think so," she added. "There was nobody left to ask when I came out. They stopped bringing me food; that's how I realised something had happened. But it took me a while to notice. By the time I came out to check, more than a week had passed."

"How did you know it was the bandits who did it?" said Tet Sang.

Guet Imm's expression did not change. "Some of their bodies were still there. My sisters fought back also."

There was a brief silence.

"But why the bandits did it, that's what I think only," said Guet Imm. "People in town didn't want to talk about what happened. Maybe they didn't know. So, I'm still not sure."

"I told you," said Tet Sang. "A silent war."

He sat down next to Guet Imm.

"It's dangerous for people to talk," he said. "They're caught between the Protectorate and the bandits. Don't blame them."

"I don't."

Tet Sang glanced at the nun. Sombre, Guet Imm looked unlike herself. "Or yourself."

"I don't," said Guet Imm. Her eyes were as dark and clear as a pool of water at night. "I don't blame myself, or the people who did it, or the deity. That's the difference between you and me."

Tet Sang didn't answer.

He expected Guet Imm to indulge in evangelism now that she'd extracted the sorry truth of his past. He would rather she rubbed salt into his wound, but he said nothing to forestall her; it was what she had been taught. He braced himself for platitudes, quotes from the scriptures, exhortations to return to the start of the road.

Instead, she said, "Where do you think the money went?"

Tet Sang blinked. "What money?"

"The money you were going to use to buy the rice, from the last job," said Guet Imm. "And the deposit Yeoh Thean Tee paid for the tokong treasures."

"Oh," said Tet Sang, nonplussed. "Some of it would have gone on the rice. Ah Lau doesn't like to owe people money." For all his faults, Fung Cheung was scrupulous in his dealings with tradespeople—the ordinary men and women living on a knife's edge in this time of war. "The rest he probably gambled away."

"I thought you said he didn't like to owe people money."

Tet Sang shrugged. "Depends on the people."

Guet Imm was gazing straight ahead, her face grave. It was hard to tell what she was thinking.

"The Yeoh family," she said, after a pause. "They're good people, followers of the deity?"

"The Yeohs are running dogs," said Tet Sang.

At Guet Imm's startled look, he said, "You cannot stay rich in times like these without eating sin. If you don't dare to do wrong, then you will suffer. There were one thousand guests at Yeoh Thean Tee's son's wedding. They had suckling pig and a separate tent just for halal food. You tell me, are they suffering?"

"That's how you think of them," said Guet Imm. "And you were willing to sell your tokong's treasures to these people?"

Tet Sang wanted to tell her that goods were not people; that everything precious in the tokong was lost beyond recovery the day the mata murdered its inhabitants. He had borne away empty things—things that had no meaning, now that those who had once polished and prayed over them were gone.

It would only have been the truth. Yet he found himself speaking another truth, emerging from a part of himself he had thought long dead and buried.

"Yeoh Thean Tee is a survivor," said Tet Sang. "After the war, whoever wins, the family will still be rich. Whether they stay here, or they run somewhere else, the Yeohs will be okay."

"They were the safest custodians you could think of," said Guet Imm.

Tet Sang looked away from the radiance of her face. "We were lucky they were willing to buy. Most people won't want things taken from a tokong where the Abbot was murdered. Scared of bad luck. That's why the price was so low."

"You shouldn't let superstition devalue what you're offering, brother," said Guet Imm. She assumed a businesslike air. "You must tell Mr Yeoh the price is eight hundred cash for each sarira, and that's only because you're giving him face in this time of war. I guess you'll have to deduct the eight hundred cash deposit he already paid," she added. "But no more than that. We cannot take responsibility for the other eight hundred, since we never received it. Mr Yeoh will pay when we explain the value of what he's getting. The objects will help protect his family. The deity's grace is in them."

"What are you talking about?" said Tet Sang.

Guet Imm reached into her robes and held out her hand. On her palm lay three crystals of extraordinary translucence and beauty—chips of trapped light that seemed to illuminate the shelter. Tet Sang had last seen them nestled in the gold chalice Guet Imm had thrown at the mata's head in Sungai Tombak.

"You—" he said. "Where did you get those from?"

"You didn't think I'd throw away the sacred relics of the deity's own body?" said Guet Imm. "Three sarira! I didn't know Permatang Timbul was so blessed. I think we should ask for three taels, actually. One tael per sarira. It would be disrespectful to the deity to ask for less."

"You didn't want to sell the relics at all! You said it was an outrage!"

Guet Imm tucked the sarira away.

"Ah, but that was before I knew the whole story," she said. "Now I understand the deity's intention. She sent me to you for a reason, brother. But we shouldn't go through that Mr Ng again. He is not an enlightened man."

"The question is," said Guet Imm, "where does Yeoh Thean Tee live?"

六

"Mr Yeoh Thean Tee is not at home," said the maidservant. "He went outstation on business. Coming back in three weeks' time."

Fung Cheung and Tet Sang exchanged a look.

"Is Mr Yeoh Kok Beng around?" ventured Fung Cheung, naming Yeoh Thean Tee's eldest son.

The maidservant shook her head. "He went with Tuan Yeoh. All the sons and nephews did. There's nobody in the house." She gave Fung Cheung a melting look, expressive of both abject apology and shameless longing. "Sorry, sir."

It would not have been like Fung Cheung to fail to respond with gallantry to anyone paying tribute to his charms. Despite his disappointment, he managed to muster a winsome smile for the girl.

"It's our bad timing," he said. "Thank you, sister." He waited till she reluctantly shut the door to turn on Tet Sang and Guet Imm, the smile falling off his face.

"So, how?" demanded Fung Cheung.

It hadn't been easy to persuade him to agree to the new plan.

"Let me check I understand correctly," he'd said when Guet Imm had explained what she proposed. "You want us to go to Yeoh Thean Tee's own house and demand an audience with one of the richest and most powerful men on the peninsula. Then you want to say to Yeoh Thean Tee, *I know we almost got your man busted by the mata, but we still want to sell you the same illicit goods we offered before. But fewer of the goods. For more money.*"

"That's it," said Guet Imm, gratified by Fung Cheung's ready understanding.

"We are outlaws wanted by the Protector," said Fung Cheung. "Maybe you have not noticed, but the mata are chasing us right now. That is why we are spending so many nights in the jungle. It is not because we *enjoy* being bitten by mosquitoes and leeches. Meanwhile, Yeoh Thean Tee's business interests depend on the Protector's support. He cannot afford to be caught fraternising with bandits—"

"Yes, but we're not bandits," said Guet Imm. "Why

shouldn't Yeoh Thean Tee talk to us? It's not like we're criminals."

"Well," said Fung Cheung cautiously. "We haven't done any *bad* crimes."

"You must understand how these things work, sister," he went on, before Guet Imm could ask any questions. "Yeoh Thean Tee only deals with people like us through intermediaries. If we go to his door, we won't even have the chance to ask for money. They will straight off shoot us."

"Not if you have a nun with you," said Guet Imm.

Fung Cheung tilted his head, considering the point, but his lip stayed in its dubious curl. "Ah Sang, you think this plan can work?"

"Yeoh Thean Tee gave a daughter to the Pure Moon," said Tet Sang. "He will know how to value the deity's relics, and how to respect one of her votaries. But whether he'll forgive the debt . . ." He shrugged. "Religion is one thing, money is another."

"More to the point, brother," said Guet Imm, "do you have any other options?"

Fung Cheung met Tet Sang's eyes.

Though they had not discussed it, the obvious course of action was to disband the group, split up and go into hiding. But this was a real choice for only some of the group. You didn't become a travelling contractor if you had anywhere better to go. Most of the brothers were not good at living in ordinary society. If Fung Cheung told them to go off and look after themselves, in all likelihood they would fail.

Everyone knew this. It made the men nervous and snappish, given to sudden outbreaks of bad temper. There had been no violence yet—Fung Cheung still had a hold on his men. They trusted him, but they would endure for only so long.

"It would be a gamble," said Fung Cheung finally, and Tet Sang knew they were going to try Guet Imm's plan.

It had been a gruelling journey getting to the capital of Kempas, where Yeoh Thean Tee had his main residence. They had stuck to travelling through the jungle and managed thereby to elude the mata. But the day before they arrived at Kempas, they had just barely avoided an encounter with a regiment of bandits. The group was setting up camp for the night when Rimau, who had gone hunting, came back empty-handed and told Fung Cheung they had to move on.

"There's a party of bandits washing at the river," said Rimau. "They have a camp here. I could smell smoke from their fires. Lucky thing they didn't see me!"

He was pale. A handful of Malayu had joined the fight for the Reformist cause, but the majority of bandits were Tang and distrusted the Malayu as sympathizers with the Protectorate, if not actual collaborators. The bandits had attacked Rimau's own village on the suspicion that the villagers had been giving the mata intelligence on bandit hideouts.

But if Rimau had particular reason to be afraid, none of the group desired a meeting with the bandits. While in theory the Reformist struggle could not succeed without the support of the masses, by this time most bandits had contracted a jaundiced view of the people, regarding them as unpredictable sources of food, supplies and betrayal. This made bandits difficult to deal with.

It had not improved the men's mood to be told they could not rest after a long, sweaty, leech-infested day hacking their way through inhospitable forest, because they must run from the bandits. They were in no temper to be told that their march to Kempas had ended in failure—there was no Yeoh Thean Tee to be appealed to.

Fung Cheung had swallowed his own disappointment by the time he made the announcement to the group. He put on a tolerable pretence of regarding Yeoh Thean Tee's absence as a small matter. "He's only gone for three weeks. We can make the deal when he comes back."

"But in the meantime, how?" demanded Ah Yee. "We're supposed to hang around in the bushes for three weeks?"

Fung Cheung gave him a look of surprise. "You thought what, we were going to check in to an inn?"

Rimau snorted, but none of the other men so much as smiled, even Ah Hin.

"This is too much, brother," said Ah Yee. "My mosquito bites have mosquito bites. Suffering for a purpose I don't mind, but who says Mr Yeoh will pay us even when he comes back?"

"I say," said Fung Cheung, unruffled. "You worry too much, Ah Yee." He reached into his robes and produced a bag, which jingled as he threw it at Ah Yee.

Ah Yee caught it, startled.

"These mosquito bites are making you bad-tempered," said Fung Cheung. "You'd better go find a herbalist in town and buy some medicine. There's a cream in a green pot that's very good, my mother used to use. Get us a good dinner while you're at it. Even if we're hiding in the bushes like bandits, there's no reason we should eat like them—living off stale rice and ideology."

"Thank you, brother," stammered Ah Yee. No one had been allowed into any town or village since Sungai Tombak. "Can Ah Wing come with me to help carry?"

Fung Cheung waved his hand. "Whatever. Just make sure you get us chicken. I'm sick of eating musang."

Tet Sang waited till the men had dispersed to their various tasks to say to Fung Cheung: "Was that a good idea?"

They'd stayed away from inhabited areas precisely to avoid the mata, and Kempas was the heart of the Protectorate's domain in the Southern Seas, the centre from which they administered the affairs of the peninsula and its neighbouring islands.

"Ah Yee is getting jumpy. Better to give him face than have a problem," said Fung Cheung. "Kempas is the last place the Protectorate will be hunting for bandits. You've seen the mata here. They all look like clerks."

Tet Sang gave him a doubtful look, but Fung Cheung sighed.

"Don't nag me, Ah Sang," he said. "I'm doing the best I can."

"What happens when all the men want money and a trip to town?"

Fung Cheung raised his hands in a gesture of helplessness. "We'll have to ask your deity then. Maybe Sister Guet Imm can intervene with the goddess on our behalf."

Your deity was a slip, a sign of Fung Cheung's state of mind. He was the only one of the men who knew about Tet Sang's past—the only one who had an idea of the circumstances in which Tet Sang had left his tokong—and he would not usually have been so tactless.

Tet Sang suppressed his wince. It might have been Fung Cheung who had decided to let Guet Imm come with them, but it was Tet Sang who had said she should stay—he who had endorsed her plan to approach Yeoh Thean Tee directly. He felt responsible for their position.

Guet Imm was conscious that she was under a cloud. She made herself scarce for most of the day, reappearing only in the evening with a basket of herbs and vegetables. When Ah Yee was predictably late returning to camp, she insisted on cooking dinner as a peace offering.

The men had not lost all their affection for her. It was

testament to their good nature that they allowed this, and ate the results with minimal apparent disgust.

They were partway through dinner when Ah Yee and Ah Wing reappeared. Tet Sang glanced at them and put down his bowl.

Fung Cheung only took notice of others' moods when it suited him. He raised his eyebrows. "No chicken, Ah Yee?"

Ah Yee's expression was thunderous. Ah Wing said, glancing nervously at him, "We had to give it to the mata."

"Ah," said Fung Cheung gently. He had already been regretting the indulgence he had shown Ah Yee. Tet Sang could tell that this new turn aggravated him. He would shortly grow scathing.

"What happened?" said Tet Sang.

Ah Yee wouldn't answer. He put down the provisions they had bought, sitting heavily on a log.

"Ah Yee bumped into a man outside the broth—outside the shop," said Ah Wing. "Turned out to be a mata. He got angry, started threatening this and that. Said he wanted to arrest us. We had to give him the chicken to get him to let us go."

"Should have given him Ah Yee," said Fung Cheung.

"Why did the mata want to arrest you?" said Tet Sang, speaking over him. "Did he recognise you all?"

It seemed unlikely. Ah Yee and Ah Wing had not appeared on the wanted posters identifying Lau Fung Cheung and his men as enemies of the Protectorate. It was true both Ah Yee and Ah Wing had been convicts before they had joined the group, but they had done their time.

Ah Wing shook his head. "The mata wanted to pick a fight only. He was drunk."

"He wasn't the only one," said Fung Cheung, looking at Ah Yee.

Ah Yee did in fact smell of beer, as did Ah Wing, but Fung Cheung could have expected nothing else when he gave them money and permission to go to town. It was injudicious of him to take out his displeasure about his own bad decision-making on Ah Yee. Tet Sang shot him a warning look.

"Maybe we were not so polite before we realised he was a mata," conceded Ah Wing. "But it was okay in the end. He was very happy about the chicken."

Fung Cheung was evidently not done making jibes. But before he could think of any more, Ah Yee spoke.

"The girl saw from the window," he said. He must have had more to drink than Ah Wing; his voice was thick. "She laughed at me."

"So what?" said Fung Cheung. "Can't be the first time a woman has laughed at you."

Ah Yee raised his head, frowning. His gaze caught on Guet Imm, who was serving out rice porridge for Ah Wing. She sensed his eyes on her and looked up.

"You want dinner, brother?" she said.

Ah Yee rose unsteadily to his feet and glared at the pot of porridge.

"You call that dinner?" said Ah Yee. "I could shit out a better meal than this!" He tried to kick the pot but missed. He stumbled, swearing.

Guet Imm didn't appear to notice that he had been offensive. "That means you want or don't want?"

Ah Yee said to Ah Wing, "What's the use of a woman if she cannot cook? Since we let this one join us, she has only caused trouble. Travel here, travel there, it's all because of her. Now we have no money and no peace. Even our blood the leeches and mosquitoes have drunk up already."

Holding his bowl of porridge, Ah Wing gave Guet Imm a look of acute embarrassment. He stammered, "There's no need to say so much, brother . . ."

"At least if she fucked us like Ah Boon wanted, it might be worth keeping her," said Ah Yee. "As it is, bringing her along is wasting rice only."

"Don't bring me into this," snapped Ah Boon. "That was before I knew Sister Guet Imm. She is a nun. How can you blame her for not fucking people? It's like if I blame you for not knowing how to behave. We all knew you're a samseng when you joined. What else can we expect?"

Ah Boon was angry enough that he asked Guet Imm for a second serving of her rice porridge. She ladled out a bowl for him, keeping an eye on Ah Yee. Her face was open, a little puzzled: *Why is brother so grouchy?* she seemed to be wondering.

But her body language belied her expression. Her entire person was tense, ready to spring.

"You're on her side because you hope she'll change her mind," said Ah Yee. He turned to Guet Imm. "You should give him a chance. Ah Boon's dick is so small, it's not like he even counts as a man."

"Ah Yee," said Tet Sang. "That's enough."

Ah Yee rolled his reddened eyes at him. "Why? You also want, is it? You should think twice, Second Brother. You'll have to take turns with Ah Boon, and you don't know how many cows he's fucked."

"I've said so many times already, it's zero!" said Ah Boon.

"The only people who've been taking turns with people are you and Ah Wing," said Fung Cheung to Ah Yee. "If it's going to make you so ill-mannered, Sister Guet Imm won't need to chop off your dick. I'll do it for her. You don't want me to be tempted, you'd better stop talking nonsense."

His tone made the men steal surreptitious looks at one another, like children reprimanded by a teacher.

In any other mood, Ah Yee would have known to stop and take himself off. But beer and his sense of grievance, solidified over the past several days, overcame his discretion.

"We give the woman too much face," he persisted. "If Second Brother hadn't taken her along to Sungai Tombak, we'd have our money by now." He jabbed a finger in Tet Sang's chest, making Tet Sang stagger. "You're the one who didn't want her to join in the first place. Why did you change your mind? She sucked your dick, is it?"

Ah Yee's jab had really been more of a shove. *He wants to piss you off,* Tet Sang reminded himself.

"Go to sleep, Ah Yee," he said, swallowing his irritation.

But it was too late. The moment Ah Yee had touched Tet Sang, Guet Imm had put down her ladle.

"You and Brother Lau are really good, brother," she said to Tet Sang, in a honeyed voice. "The way you take pity on the soft-minded, the deity will surely reward you!"

Ah Yee said, "You mean the deity will—"

"No, I don't mean she will grant sexual favours, brother," said Guet Imm serenely. "The Pure Moon is a goddess, you know. You mustn't confuse her with the girl who laughed at you today when you were grovelling to the mata. That must have been very embarrassing!"

"Shut up!" growled Ah Yee. He cuffed her—or tried to. Guet Imm caught his wrist.

"Ah Yee!" said Fung Cheung, half-rising, but Tet Sang was looking at Guet Imm.

"Sister," he said in a warning tone.

But this was the excuse Guet Imm had been waiting for. She ignored him.

"Oh, brother, that was a bad idea!" she said softly, shining eyes fixed on Ah Yee.

Ah Yee screamed, yanking back his arm, but Guet Imm wouldn't let him go. He shoved his other hand into his robe. When it emerged, it held a blade.

The men were all on their feet.

"Come, brother, enough already," said Ah Wing, hovering apprehensively behind Ah Yee. "There's no need for all this!"

"Sister, get back!" shouted Ah Hin.

"I am going to chop off *everybody's* dicks!" snarled Fung Cheung.

Guet Imm did not seem to notice the noise. When Ah Yee lunged at her, he found she was no longer there. She pinned his arm behind his back and slipped the knife out of his hand.

"Argh!" said Ah Yee. He twisted around, his face purple. "Go and die, you fucking whore, and your precious deity too!"

Guet Imm elbowed him forcefully in the side. As he gasped, she hit the back of his neck, downing him. Once he was on the ground, she kicked him in the stomach for good measure.

"Sister, that's enough," said Tet Sang. To immobilise

Ah Yee was one thing, but that last kick had been pure spite.

But Guet Imm wasn't listening, to him or the others, who were each loudly articulating his opinion on what she should do or stop doing. She dropped to her knees, seized Ah Yee by the forelock and pulled back his head. Firelight gleamed off metal as she raised the blade she had taken from him.

It was not the time to remind Guet Imm of the Pure Moon's decrees against unnecessary violence. Tet Sang grabbed Guet Imm's arm, squeezing mercilessly. When she loosened her grip in surprise, he snatched the knife out of her hand.

"I said, *that's enough,*" he said.

"Quiet, all of you," he added over his shoulder to everyone else. "They could hear you from Kempas! You want the mata to come and catch us?"

Guet Imm was still clutching Ah Yee's hair as though she was considering simply breaking his neck now that Tet Sang had deprived her of the knife. He had no doubt she could do it.

"He insulted the deity!" she said.

"So what?" said Tet Sang. "She's a goddess. What does Ah Yee's insult matter to her? If she wants to punish him, let her punish. For humans, she set limits. You are about to go over."

Everything Tet Sang said was unarguable according to the doctrines of the Order. Still, Guet Imm wavered. "None of the deity's rules are set in stone. You're allowed to exercise discretion."

Tet Sang gave this sophistry the attention it deserved. "You've done enough, sister. Let Ah Yee go."

After a moment, Guet Imm released Ah Yee's head, letting it drop to the ground. A groan confirmed that Ah Yee was conscious, but—with the most sense he'd shown that evening—he stayed still while Guet Imm stormed off.

Ah Hin made an aborted movement, as though he was thinking of following her, but Tet Sang caught Fung Cheung's eyes and shook his head.

"Never mind her," said Fung Cheung. "Someone help Ah Yee. Ah Boon, go and have a look at him."

"He said I fucked cows," protested Ah Boon.

But Fung Cheung had exhausted his fund of patience for the day.

"Who hasn't said you fuck cows?" he snapped. "We've all said it. You want to be sensitive, you can go find another group. You all are too much. Any more and I'll report us to the mata myself. At least then I might get some peace!"

Ah Wing helped Ah Yee to sit up. Ah Boon went to tend to him, grumbling under his breath. The others started tidying up—a fair amount of rice porridge had got distributed across the camp in the course of the quarrel.

Fung Cheung turned to Tet Sang.

"What the hell was that?" said Fung Cheung.

———

Guet Imm was sitting cross-legged in the shelter Ah Hin had built for her, her hands folded. The uninitiated might have thought she was meditating.

"You're sulking," said Tet Sang.

"Where got?" said Guet Imm sulkily.

Conscious that this was less than convincing, she retreated into aloof silence. Her bad mood was palpable—Tet Sang could almost see the black cloud above her head.

Tet Sang stood for a while, considering his course of action, then sat down on a convenient bundle. He allowed himself to grimace while he did it, though there was merely a slight twinge from his wound.

Guet Imm glared at him.

"The relics are in there," she said.

Tet Sang looked down at the mud-stained bundle. It was something of a comedown for the sarira from having been cherished in a gold goblet, but, "They'll survive," he said.

Guet Imm could hardly disagree, since orthodoxy held that the relics of the Pure Moon were indestructible, harder than diamond. Besides, his grimace had bothered her. She kept her meditation pose for a few more seconds, stealing looks under lowered lashes at Tet

Sang, while he enjoyed the novel sensation of being the unflustered one.

Eventually, Guet Imm snapped.

"You're hurt," she said. "Did Brother Ah Yee poke your wound? I knew it!"

Tet Sang waved a dismissive hand. "It's itchy only."

"Let me look at it," said Guet Imm.

Changing the dressing calmed her down. The black cloud dispersed. It left Guet Imm far from penitent but—Tet Sang thought—in a state that could be worked on.

"Ah Lau wants you to say sorry to Ah Yee," he said.

Guet Imm's head whipped up. "Say sorry for what? Brother Ah Yee's the one who started it!"

"I'm not saying it's fair," said Tet Sang. "But a group like this is like a family. It's important to maintain harmony. Ah Yee is under pressure. His mother is not well. His sister is a widow with children. If we don't find some way to get the money, his relatives will not eat."

Guet Imm was not impressed. "Would he like men to talk to his mother and sister the way he talked today?"

"If you want to say Ah Yee doesn't know how to behave, that's true," said Tet Sang. "But when did he have the chance to learn? You are different. You've had advantages he's never had."

"The deity speaks to everyone," said Guet Imm defiantly. "It's whether they want to hear or not."

Tet Sang waited while she washed her hands and dried them, scowling.

Finally she said, "You think I should apologise."

"Who cares what I think? You're the one who sat in a cell for how many years thinking about right and wrong," said Tet Sang. "What do *you* think you should do?"

Guet Imm looked furious. The youngest novice of the Order of the Pure Moon could have told them that according to the deity's precepts, it was for Guet Imm to bow her head and forget her ego.

"I wasn't thinking about right or wrong when I was in seclusion," she retorted. "I wasn't thinking about anything. That's the point of meditation. You're supposed to empty your mind."

"You're right, of course," said Tet Sang mildly.

Guet Imm glowered at him some more. "If I don't say sorry, then what? Brother Lau will kick me out?"

Tet Sang shrugged. "It's Ah Lau's group. It's for him to decide."

Guet Imm shook out her sleeves, raising her head with the air of a martyr. "If I have to say sorry or he'll kick me out, then there's no choice. I have nowhere else to go." She shot Tet Sang a vengeful look, daring him to say anything about coffeehouses.

But having won his point, Tet Sang had no interest in gloating. "Thank you, sister. Sometimes, we all have to sacrifice to keep the peace." He paused, then added, "Ah Lau might ask about your martial arts training."

Guet Imm had turned, as though she meant to charge out and get the apology over with right then. She looked back. "What about it?"

"The men were surprised you knew how to fight." Tet Sang examined his grubby nails dispassionately.

Guet Imm blinked. "Really? Don't they know *anything* about the Order?"

Tet Sang hummed. "You'll be surprised what people know—or think they know. There's been," he said deliberately, "some talk about witchcraft."

"Oh?" said Guet Imm. "And what did you say?"

It was the first time that evening that Tet Sang found it hard to decipher her expression. But simplicity had served him well so far.

"I cannot say what I don't know," he said. "I was not an anchorite. Even—back then—these things were closed to me."

Guet Imm sat back down, frowning.

"Shaping the earth is one thing," she said. She was referring to the five key devotional practices of followers of the Pure Moon—the five fingers of the goddess's hand. The first: emptying the gourd with meditation. The second: filling the gourd with the chanting of scriptures. The third: planting seeds by analysing the scriptures. The fourth: shaping the earth by cultivating one's physical powers. And the fifth: shaping the air by cultivating one's spiritual powers. The last included the practice of the healing arts but also other arts which were rather more obscure. Laypeople called these magic.

All five fingers were regarded as divine mysteries, to each of which a votary could productively devote a lifetime. But that did not mean there was no hierarchy.

"I can tell them how I learnt to fight," said Guet Imm. "But the fifth finger of the deity's hand . . . that is a deep matter. Even if I know how to explain, will they know how to understand?"

"Not much scares the men," said Tet Sang. "But who is comfortable when it comes to witchcraft? I cannot tell you what to say, sister. But if it's Ah Lau who asks, I think it's best to give him some kind of answer. To say nothing will make people nervous, and frightened men behave badly. You saw Ah Yee tonight."

Guet Imm's face fell. "Is it so easy for them to distrust me? I've done my best for you all, brother. Can you say I didn't contribute? Try and smell Brother Ah Hin!"

"We all smell better," Tet Sang reassured her. "Don't get me wrong. The men are still your friends. I am just saying, be careful. Most of them are not in a good situation. Otherwise, they wouldn't have become roving contractors.

"Everyone knows we cannot risk waiting three weeks for Yeoh Thean Tee to come back. The only place to hide from the mata is the jungle. But if we stay here, how are we supposed to hide from the bandits? Right now, the men are disappointed. It won't take much to make them desperate."

"Oh, we won't have to wait three weeks," said Guet Imm. "I know what we can do. I would have told Brother Lau if not for all the disturbance."

Tet Sang stared. "What?"

"It's not like only Yeoh Thean Tee has keys to the Yeoh family vault," said Guet Imm. "There are other people in the family."

"The maid told us everyone went on this business trip."

"No, she told us Yeoh Thean Tee's sons and nephews went with him," said Guet Imm. "But when she said there was nobody in the house, that made me wonder who counted as somebody. I thought, *Surely, Yeoh Thean Tee didn't take his wife and mother along.* So, I went back to his house in the afternoon—"

"You *what?*"

"Don't worry. I didn't talk to anybody but the servants," said Guet Imm. "It was a good thing I went back; they gave me the vegetables for our dinner. Otherwise, we would have had to eat white rice. And they told me Grandmother and Mrs Yeoh were at home, along with all the daughters-in-law and nieces and whatnot—all the women."

"So what?"

"Well, at first I thought Grandmother was promising," said Guet Imm. "Even Yeoh Thean Tee must listen to his mother. But apparently, her father was a foreigner and she prays at the Protectorate's churches. I was very disappointed, but then the maids told me something interesting. Remember I told you about Yeoh Gaik Tin?"

Tet Sang didn't, but nevertheless the name sounded familiar. He searched his memory. "You mean Yeoh Thean Tee's daughter? The acolyte?"

"We called her Sister Anitya," said Guet Imm.

"She was at *your tokong*?" said Tet Sang. "You didn't tell me that!"

"I did," insisted Guet Imm. "I told you, Yeoh Thean Tee paid for our turtle pond."

This, Tet Sang did recollect. "You didn't say it was because his daughter was a novice at your tokong."

"Why else would Yeoh Thean Tee buy us a turtle pond?" said Guet Imm.

This was unanswerable, and Tet Sang was not interested in answering it anyway. A horrible thought had struck him. "You said there was nobody left alive from your tokong." If their hopes of payment depended on a nun of the very Order that had been involved in the death of Yeoh Thean Tee's daughter, they were finished.

"Oh, nobody who was still there," said Guet Imm. "But you know rich people, brother; they stay for a short time only. Sister Anitya left the Order when I was in seclusion, long before the bandits came. She's married now. She could help us."

It seemed highly unlikely to Tet Sang that a man like Yeoh Thean Tee would pay any regard to the opinions of a daughter, and he said so.

"There's no way she'll have authority to forgive the debt," he said. "If we try to negotiate with her, Yeoh Thean Tee will simply send his men after us to take back whatever she gives us. Then not only will we be in debt to him, we'll be the people who tried to con his daughter."

"You don't know Sister Anitya," said Guet Imm. "I did. She could make the deal for us."

"So, you want to ask her," said Tet Sang. When Guet Imm nodded, he said, with a vision of how Fung Cheung would look when he was recommended another fruitless quest, "And where does she live?"

"Kempas," said Guet Imm triumphantly. "The husband left his family to join hers. See?"

It wasn't unheard of for the son of a lower-status family to be absorbed into his wife's household and lineage instead of the other way around. But . . . "Didn't Yeoh Gaik Tin marry a rich man?"

"Chuah Siaw Loon. He's a timber tycoon," said Guet Imm. "It wasn't a matter of money or name. It's Sister Anitya's character. If she wants to make the deal, it will happen. I just need to talk to her. If she's anything like she was at the tokong, she will help."

Tet Sang opened his mouth to protest, though he could feel his scepticism crumbling in the face of her certainty.

Guet Imm was nothing like the Abbot at Permatang Timbul in almost every respect, but she shared with the Abbot the rare quality of a faith so potent that it gave off its own heat and light, dazzling onlookers. It was impossible not to trust that things would be as she said.

"This war has changed us all, sister," he said, but it was the final gambit of one who knew himself defeated.

"The deity led us here," said Guet Imm. "She won't fail us. Let me try."

They spoke to Fung Cheung, but Tet Sang thought it neither necessary nor advisable to inform the rest of the group about Guet Imm's intention to attempt to parley with Yeoh Thean Tee's daughter. Yet somehow, the news spread anyway.

The next morning, Ah Boon said to him, "The plan, with the Yeoh daughter . . . is it a good idea, Second Brother?"

There was no point asking how Ah Boon had heard of the plan. For all their differences, the brothers were united in their hatred of informers.

"You don't like it?" said Tet Sang.

"Sister Guet Imm has good intentions," said Ah Boon. "But why would Yeoh Thean Tee listen to his daughter, even if she asks him to forgive our debt? Anyway, most likely this daughter will simply call the mata on us. Then how?"

All of these points and more had occurred to Tet Sang. He'd expected Fung Cheung to rehearse the same arguments when Guet Imm presented the proposal to him the night before. Instead, Fung Cheung had said, "Why not? No doubt you will make an offering to your goddess before you go to see this woman, sister."

"The deity will look after us," said Guet Imm.

Fung Cheung nodded.

Tet Sang said dubiously, "You think it's a good plan?"

"Oh, no. I think the plan makes no sense," said Fung Cheung. "But to tell the truth, Ah Sang, I don't know what to do also." He raised his eyes to the sky. The full moon rode low among the clouds, giving off a white glow as pure as the light of the goddess's face was said to be. "Since we are here anyway, it's worth a shot. Who knows? Maybe Fate will give us a break."

Here was the power of Guet Imm's faith again, thought Tet Sang—or in other words, the power of superstition.

They decided that Guet Imm and Tet Sang would pay the visit. At least if they were hauled off by the mata, Fung Cheung would not be involved.

"Even if she sent us away, Sister Anitya wouldn't do

that," said Guet Imm, but she didn't object to it being the two of them. "I don't think Brother Lau's face would make much difference to her. She is not the kind to be swayed by that sort of thing."

But Fung Cheung's approval did little to lighten the atmosphere in the camp. Ah Yee was morose, despite the apology Guet Imm had made, and he was not the only one who was unhappy. A lingering discontent hung over the men.

"That woman has spoilt our peace," said Rimau.

If this troubled Guet Imm, she did not show it. It seemed to be Tet Sang alone who felt himself to be on a fool's mission when they set off for Yeoh Gaik Tin's house. He tried to comfort himself with the thought that Yeoh Gaik Tin must indeed be an unusual person, if she was living with neither her husband's nor her own family but had set up her own household.

It was an elderly woman who opened the door. She looked them over, frowning. From her aged samfu, she appeared to be an old retainer.

Tet Sang had left behind his parang and borrowed Fung Cheung's second-best set of robes. From the neck down, he looked respectable, even prosperous: "You could be a sundry shop owner," said Guet Imm approvingly.

But there was nothing to be done about Tet Sang's face. It clearly did not strike the maidservant as the face of a sundry shop owner. Her expression did not grow any more welcoming when her eyes moved to Guet Imm.

"Yes, I'm sure you want to see the mistress of the house," she said when Guet Imm repeated her request. "A lot of nuns and monks want to see Madam Yeoh. But who are you?"

Guet Imm glanced at Tet Sang.

"I'm an old friend," she said. "Tell her it's Sister Nirodha. She will remember me."

The maidservant snorted. "You'll be surprised how many con artists in mendicant robes are 'old friends' of Madam Yeoh. She spent five years in that tokong, and apparently she met every religious on the peninsula. I suppose you'll say you are also from the Order of the Pure Moon?"

"Auntie, what else can I say but the truth?" said Guet Imm, wide-eyed. "I won't say I was Madam Yeoh's good friend—"

"Ha!"

"But I really knew her," Guet Imm continued. "Please, can't you ask her and see what she says?"

The old retainer glared at her. "So, you're not here to beg for money?"

If Tet Sang had thought Guet Imm would be tripped up by this, or even blush, he had thought too little of her (or perhaps too much). She drew herself up, the picture of outraged innocence.

"Beg for money! Auntie, these other nuns and monks who came may not have been sincere, but you must not judge my heart by such people. I have travelled for days so I can see Sister Anitya's face again."

"Who are these people, Second Aunt?" said a new voice.

A woman stood at the bottom of the steps leading to the main door. She wore an Occidental-style dress, expensively simple, with gold bangles on her wrists and jade drops in her ears. She gave an overmastering impression of elegance—an elegance that had no need of youth or beauty, since it had its source in power.

"Who else? More of your beggars," said the elderly woman, evidently no retainer after all. "This girl says she knows you, Ah Tin."

Yeoh Gaik Tin raised a perfect eyebrow. "But I don't know her."

Guet Imm gave her a burning look of betrayal. "Oh, Sister Anitya!"

"I told you and your father so many times already," said the aunt. "So long as you give people money, they will keep coming. You cannot feed every monk and nun in the country."

Yeoh Gaik Tin said to Guet Imm, "How did you know my Ascended name?" But then her eyes met Tet Sang's. They widened.

"We were at the same tokong, sister," said Guet Imm. "I'm Sister Guet Imm; Nirodha was my Ascended name. Don't you remember? I'm sure we overlapped for a year. Six months at the very least!"

Yeoh Gaik Tin was not listening. Her hand had flown to her mouth.

"Sister Khanti!" she said. She went up the steps, reaching out, but stopped short of touching Tet Sang. She stood gazing at him as though he were a precious object—a marvel she had not thought to see. "You survived!"

———

"This is a great blessing," said Yeoh Gaik Tin. "I heard the Permatang Timbul tokong was destroyed. Everybody there, gone."

They were seated in a parlour opening on the central courtyard of Madam Yeoh's mansion. Tet Sang nodded awkwardly at the servant pouring him tea. Guet Imm's eyes were burning holes into the side of his head.

"Why you didn't say you knew Yeoh Gaik Tin?" she'd whispered as Madam Yeoh had whisked them into the house.

"I *don't* know her!" said Tet Sang.

"She seems to know you!"

Certainly, Madam Yeoh's hospitality suggested some prior acquaintance. The moment they sat down, servants poured forth from parts unknown, covering the blackwood table with a bounty of kuih. Guet Imm ate three in rapid succession, while Tet Sang sat with his palms pressed against his thighs. The aunt who had greeted them retired from the scene, grumbling.

"But you escaped, Sister Khanti," said Yeoh Gaik Tin. She clasped her hands. "This is all thanks to Heaven!"

Tet Sang had racked his brains but could not unearth any familiarity with the name *Anitya*. It was unnerving. His problem had always been that he remembered too much about the Order, not too little. Perhaps his efforts to forget had been more successful than he had thought.

"Yes," he said. "I escaped. And you, sister . . . were you at Permatang Timbul also?"

A cloud passed over Yeoh Gaik Tin's face. "You don't remember me!"

Tet Sang coughed. "Well . . ."

"No, no. There's no reason you should," said Yeoh Gaik Tin. "I was at a different tokong."

"The tokong at Bukit Hitam," said Guet Imm. "I was there also."

"Ah, really?" said Madam Yeoh, glancing at Guet Imm without recognition. "Very good! Welcome, sister."

She turned back to Tet Sang. "Yes, I was at the Bukit Hitam tokong. I joined a delegation to Permatang Timbul in the year 2483. I attended your lecture on the Clear Heart scriptures. Wah!" She shook her head. "I'll never forget it. It was like drinking from a spring of fresh water."

Guet Imm's fiery gaze intensified. "You gave lectures?" she said to Tet Sang.

"That was one of sister's earliest lectures," said Yeoh Gaik Tin. "It was only later on that she became famous for them." She said to Tet Sang, "I attended as a layperson when you came to Kempas also. That was after I'd left my tokong. But that time, I had no chance to speak to you. There were too many people there."

"I thought you were a novice," said Guet Imm, indignant. "You said the mysteries were closed to you!"

"I said I didn't know anything about shaping the air," Tet Sang corrected her. "I focused on the scriptures. Anyone can read the scriptures with training."

"But few could explain them the way you did, sister," said Yeoh Gaik Tin, in a tone of reproof. "Even the elders admired you. My Abbot had all your exegeses in her study."

Tet Sang inclined his head in acknowledgment of the compliment.

"It was a long time ago," he said, with—he hoped—more composure than he felt. "A lot of things have happened since then. Please don't call me *sister*, Madam Yeoh. I am not a member of the Order anymore. That title is not for me."

Yeoh Gaik Tin looked at him, taking in, for perhaps the first time, the long hair and the men's robes. The light in her eyes faded.

"Yes," she said. "A lot of things have happened these past few years. I am sorry, sis—I am sorry. I shouldn't have talked so carelessly about the past."

Tet Sang shook his head. "It is good Madam Yeoh is

not scared of speaking about such things. Sister Nirodha and I have come on a mission from the past."

He glanced at Guet Imm. She glared back at him, as much as to say, *We're not done talking about this.* But she said nothing, reaching into her robes and drawing out a small bag, which she offered to Yeoh Gaik Tin.

Madam Yeoh took the bag, opening it. She shook the sarira out onto her palm.

Her eyes widened. "But these are . . ."

"The relics of the deity," said Tet Sang. "The most precious treasures of my tokong, and the only ones that remain. The rest have been confiscated."

He told her an edited version of the events that had led them to her door, including their agreement with her father and the ambush by the mata at Sungai Tombak.

"They took everything? The statue also?" said Madam Yeoh. "I remember that statue. It was the one in your Abbot's room, right? Beautiful work! The Protector will send it back to his country, but his countrymen won't know how to appreciate."

The thought seemed to pain her. She put a hand to her temple. "So many things have been lost."

"But much has survived," said Guet Imm. There was a note in her voice that made Yeoh Gaik Tin raise her eyes. "It was not coincidence that we managed to save the sarira, Sister Anitya, or that we found our way to you."

Yeoh Gaik Tin looked thoughtful.

"Your Abbot at Permatang Timbul," she said to Tet Sang. "She died?"

"Yes," said Tet Sang. "She would have wanted these kept somewhere safe. Looked after by one of the faithful."

Yeoh Gaik Tin had all the character Guet Imm had credited her with. She asked no more questions, but said, "How much do you want?"

Before Tet Sang could speak, Guet Imm blurted:

"Six silver taels. Two per sarira. Minus the eight hundred cash, of course, which your father paid us already."

Tet Sang swallowed the urge to object—it was too late now in any event. Guet Imm went on:

"It is impossible to put a price on these relics, as you know, sister. Whoever holds them will have the deity's protection. That's no small thing in these times. To ask for ten taels also would not be too much. But since you were a follower of the Order, and you knew the Abbot, the deity will not mind if we give you face."

Guet Imm spoke with a decent facsimile of her habitual irritating serenity. But Tet Sang saw that the knuckles on her hands, folded in her lap, were white.

Madam Yeoh was silent for a long moment, looking from Guet Imm to Tet Sang and back again.

At least it was unlikely that she would call the mata to kick them out, what with the welcome she had given them and her open acknowledgment of having been a devotee of the Pure Moon. It would probably be private guards, who would not rough them up too much so long as they went quietly. That would be fine. Even Guet Imm was not so stupid as to fight the Yeoh family's private guards.

"Six taels," said Madam Yeoh. She shook her head, smiling slightly. "You are trying to cheat me, sister!"

Guet Imm's eyes widened. Tet Sang wished he had taken a kuih. Hearing the name they had called him at his tokong—*Sister Khanti*—had chased away hunger, but now that they were shortly to be sent packing, he felt he had been foolish to miss the opportunity.

"Cheat you, sister?" Guet Imm began, all ingenuous indignation.

"That's what I would say if this was a business matter," said Madam Yeoh. "But this is not business. Money is not important, compared to preserving the light of the Pure Moon. I will pay what you ask and be glad to have the honour of keeping the sarira safe—if you will do me a favour."

Guet Imm seemed as taken aback by the success of her feint as Tet Sang. It took her a moment to recover her composure. "Of course. Anything we can do to help . . ."

Madam Yeoh looked at Tet Sang.

"Will you stay?" she said.

———

"Didn't go well, is it?" said Fung Cheung. He clapped Tet Sang on the shoulder. "Never mind. No harm trying."

The rest of the group hovered nearby, affecting to be occupied with various tasks, but that was just as well. It would save making a second announcement.

Tet Sang set down the bag Madam Yeoh had given them. It clinked, making the brothers' heads rise.

"Ten per cent down payment from Yeoh Gaik Tin," said Tet Sang. "She'll pay six taels for the relics, minus the eight hundred cash we owe her father. Her people will give us the rest tomorrow if we bring some men to help carry."

"Six taels . . ." Fung Cheung ripped open the bag. Strings of cash tumbled out. The brothers abandoned all pretence of not listening, crowding around.

Fung Cheung swore. "You left the goods with this Yeoh Gaik Tin?"

Guet Imm opened her hand to show him the sarira. "She'll get them when the balance is paid."

"And she agreed to this deal?" said Fung Cheung incredulously. He sat back on his heels, shaking his head. "You've done it again, Ah Sang. I thought we'd have to turn ourselves in to the Protectorate to escape Yeoh Thean Tee's men. Instead, you've made us rich!"

"It was Sister Guet Imm's idea," said Tet Sang.

"You're the one who made the deal, brother," said Guet Imm.

Neither of them was especially cheerful, but Fung Cheung was too amazed by their windfall to take notice.

"Six taels for a few pebbles!" he marvelled. "The woman must be crazy."

"Who knew there were still such pious people in the world?" said Ah Hin. He gave Guet Imm a shining look. "This good luck is because of sister. Madam Yeoh would never agree to pay so much if anyone else asked."

Guet Imm glanced at Tet Sang. When he stayed silent, she said, "Actually, the six taels is not just for the relics."

"The sarira are a great treasure," Madam Yeoh had said. "But the living light of the Pure Moon is embodied in her votaries."

She gazed at her courtyard with its graceful blossoming plants, her face troubled.

"These days, it is hard to know how to be a person," she said. "To avoid doing wrong is not easy, never mind doing good. I have been praying for guidance—a light in this darkness. Now the deity has sent you to me. It's a sign."

Tet Sang looked at Guet Imm, but she had gone opaque. He could no more tell what she was thinking than one could discern what lay at the bottom of a moon-lit pond at night.

He could act as though he had not heard, or treat the proposal as a joke. But Yeoh Gaik Tin was a powerful woman doing them a great favour. What was more, she was sincere. She deserved a real answer.

"Madam Yeoh honours me," he said finally. "But I am not qualified to advise anyone, much less Madam Yeoh."

"You underrate your own powers," Madam Yeoh began, but Tet Sang raised his hand.

"You must understand. I am not being modest," he said. "I am not what Madam Yeoh thinks me. I belonged to a tokong once, yes. But that tokong is gone. Now I belong to nothing."

He braced himself for doubt, questioning, challenges. To his surprise, Yeoh Gaik Tin laughed.

"What?" said Tet Sang crossly when she didn't stop laughing.

"Sorry, sorry," said Madam Yeoh, sobering up. She lifted grave eyes to Tet Sang. "This has been a long war for everybody. Who among us has not changed? But you shouldn't need me to tell you that the deity doesn't let go of her people so easily."

She rose. Tet Sang and Guet Imm got to their feet, exchanging an uncertain look.

"I want six hundred cash for Sister Nirodha and her friend," Madam Yeoh told a servant. To Tet Sang she said, "My people can bring the rest to you if you tell me where to bring it, or you can come and pick it up tomorrow. The eight hundred cash you took already I must hold back for my father, so the balance will be four thousand, six hundred only. Do you want it in taels or cash?"

"Cash will be fine," said Guet Imm quickly. "The deity keep you in her regard, sister!"

Madam Yeoh waved away Tet Sang's stammered thanks.

"I won't call you *sister,* since you asked," she said. "But think about my offer. It is not a condition. Either way, I will pay. But Heaven wished us to meet today. These things don't happen for no reason."

Now, her eyes on Fung Cheung, Guet Imm said, "Yeoh Gaik Tin made us another offer. She wants a spiritual adviser."

Fung Cheung raised an eyebrow. "A spiritual adviser? What for?"

"To join her staff," said Tet Sang, before Guet Imm could reply. "To these rich people, piety is just one more thing to collect. A religious in the house makes them look good to their friends. So, we've agreed to supply her with a nun."

Guet Imm's head came up. "You have?"

"Sister Guet Imm is going to stay with Madam Yeoh," said Tet Sang.

"What?" said the brothers.

"*What?*" said Guet Imm.

Fung Cheung was the only one who showed no surprise. "Makes sense." Guet Imm's career interested him less than the arrangements for collecting the remaining monies from Yeoh Gaik Tin. "Tomorrow, how many people should we send? I can go also. I'm interested to meet this Madam Yeoh."

Tet Sang had no chance to answer in the clamour that rose from the others.

"Sister is leaving us?" cried Ah Boon.

"But sister, you haven't finished teaching me yet," protested Ah Hin. "There's still three more chapters of the Baby God book to go."

"What are you talking about?" Guet Imm said to Tet Sang. "Madam Yeoh wanted *you*!"

"Yeoh Gaik Tin wants a nun," said Tet Sang. "I told her already, I am not a nun. You are."

Guet Imm had lost all her usual calm. Her eyes flashing, she said, "So what, I'm supposed to turn up at her house and ask her to let me stay?"

"Why ask? Tell her you're staying," said Tet Sang. "You didn't ask when you joined us."

"And you never wanted me here," said Guet Imm in a cold fury. "You don't need to say. I know! You couldn't wait for a chance to get rid of me, and now you have it."

This was all so unlike Guet Imm that it distracted Ah Hin and Ah Boon from their distress.

"Don't be upset, sister," said Ah Hin. "You have misunderstood Second Brother. He is thinking of your benefit."

"It is a good thing for you," said Ah Boon. "Better life than being on the road, having to sleep in the jungle and run from the mata."

Guet Imm ignored them.

"But what if I don't want to go?" she said to Tet Sang. "Hah, you never thought of that, did you? You can't force me!"

Fung Cheung took it upon himself to intervene.

"Sister Guet Imm, nobody is forcing anybody," he said, in a maddeningly reasonable manner. "But if Madam Yeoh is paying us five taels plus and forgiving our debt, she must have what she wants. This is a good solution for everybody. It's not like you could have stayed with us forever. As Ah Boon says, this is no life for a nun."

"I sat alone in a cell for ten years," said Guet Imm. She was still looking at Tet Sang. "Compared to that, this cannot be considered a hard life. Of all people, you should know that, brother!"

"Enough, sister," said Tet Sang. "It is for the best."

"That's right," agreed Fung Cheung. "Ah Sang has settled everything. There's no need to argue so much. Sister Guet Imm can go to Madam Yeoh's house with the men tomorrow to deliver the relics, and then she can stay."

He turned to Tet Sang. "You and I should go tomorrow, but who else?"

Before Tet Sang could answer, Guet Imm said, "Do what you want, brother—leave me behind, get rid of the treasures, pretend you don't have a past. It won't work. You'll bring yourself along wherever you go, and the deity will find you there."

She turned on her heel and stormed off into the trees.

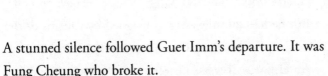

A stunned silence followed Guet Imm's departure. It was Fung Cheung who broke it.

"Women!" He shook his head. "It's time Sister Guet Imm moved on. I don't know why she's making such a fuss. If I could stay in a rich woman's house and chant scriptures for my rice, I would want also."

Tet Sang made an affirmative noise, since Fung Cheung had said this for his benefit. It did not make him feel any better, but his feelings did not matter. Nor did Guet Imm's indignation at having her fate decided for her, justified though it was.

When she calmed down, she would see this was the

right decision for both the group and herself. She was becoming the focus of the men's discontent at the hardships and misadventures that were necessary incidents of a life like theirs. In time, the resentment would inevitably spread from Ah Yee and fester, even if Guet Imm behaved herself—which seemed unlikely, given her prior record.

Tet Sang did feel some unease when Guet Imm did not return to the camp at nightfall. This was shared by Fung Cheung.

"Should have taken the sarira from her," he muttered. "The Yeoh woman said she would pay even if there was no nun, right?"

"Don't worry," said Tet Sang. "She won't have run off."

But he had a restless night, plagued by dreams of the past. The next morning, Guet Imm still had not appeared.

Ah Hin was distressed enough that he forgot the deference the brothers usually showed Fung Cheung.

"Big Brother should have been more patient," he said at breakfast. "What if Sister Guet Imm has been attacked by a wild animal?"

"Then I feel sorry for the wild animal," said Fung Cheung, but he was uneasy. He glanced at the surrounding forest into which Guet Imm had disappeared.

Ah Yee had made breakfast with his eyes downcast, apparently as oppressed by Guet Imm's absence as everyone else, but he could not resist making a contribution.

"She should know better than to go off by herself," he said. "This is the jungle, not her tokong."

Ah Hin gave him a reproachful look. "Spiritual people are sensitive. Otherwise, how can they hear the voice of the god? Sister Guet Imm has brought us good luck. If she's in trouble, it will be our fault for not looking after her."

"Sister Guet Imm can look after herself," said Tet Sang.

But in truth, Fung Cheung only echoed his thoughts when he said, "Someone should go look for her." Fung Cheung added, with a feigned air of unconcern, "We don't want to miss our appointment with Madam Yeoh."

"I'll go," said Ah Hin.

Fung Cheung nodded, glancing at Tet Sang. "Maybe you should go also, Ah Sang."

After a moment's deliberation, Tet Sang shook his head.

"I'm the one who made her angry. Sister may not want to see me. Most likely she's sulking somewhere. Better if Ah Hin goes and talks to her alone. But call us if you need help," he said to Ah Hin.

Ah Hin nodded.

He had only been gone for a short time when they heard a bloodcurdling yell from the trees.

Fung Cheung started to his feet. "Was that Ah Hin?"

The second scream removed all doubt.

"Help, help!" shrieked Ah Hin's distant voice. "Bandits!"

"You all pack up and go," said Tet Sang to Fung Cheung. "I'll go find Ah Hin and the nun."

Fung Cheung nodded. The men had already sprung into action, breaking down the camp. Without looking around, Tet Sang reached out and grabbed Ah Yee by the scruff of the neck before he could sidle away.

"You're coming with me, brother," he said.

He'd acted on a mere suspicion, but it coalesced into certainty when Ah Yee yelped, "What for? What did I do?"

"Guess we'll find out," said Tet Sang grimly. "Come on."

———

There were five bandits, all armed. One of them was holding his gun to Ah Hin's jaw.

"So, there are more of you," said the bandit. "Where's the nun?"

Tet Sang said, "What nun?"

The bandit who was holding Ah Hin hostage looked like someone's little brother—his moon-shaped face seemed too youthful for a life of armed aggression. His scowl made him look petulant rather than menacing, but there was nothing childlike about his gun or the way he yanked Ah Hin's head back. Ah Hin whimpered.

"There is a corrupt nun who plans to sell looted tokong treasures to the Yeoh family," said Little Brother. "The Yeohs are collaborators with the imperialist oppressors—running dogs of the Protectorate. Those treasures belong to the people. We've been asked to save the treasures and exact justice."

"Who asked you?" said Tet Sang, glancing at Ah Yee. Guilt was written clear across his face.

Even to vent his lingering spite against Guet Imm, it was a bizarre thing for Ah Yee to have done. He must have known that the bandits would not approve of Lau Fung Cheung's group either, as contractors who accepted jobs from both sides of the conflict. The Reformists hated businessmen.

"It wasn't me, brother!" gasped Ah Yee.

"We have people everywhere," said Little Brother. "We know everything the Yeoh family is doing."

Tet Sang thought of the servants who had poured tea and served kuih at Yeoh Gaik Tin's house. He should have thought of the risk of being overheard. If he hadn't been so taken aback by being recognised . . .

"That brother," said Little Brother, nodding at Ah Yee, "just told us where to find the nun only. And he lied! She wasn't there!"

"I didn't," said Ah Yee, wincing. "I won't dare to lie. It was a mistake!"

"Give us the nun and the treasures, and we'll let you go," said Little Brother to Tet Sang. "The brother explained the nun misled you. In the new republic, the people's faith in the gods will not be exploited in this way. To ensure this, corrupt monks and nuns must be punished."

"We will cooperate," said Tet Sang. "But we haven't

seen the nun since last night." He was watching Ah Hin's face and saw the flicker in his eyes. Luckily, the bandits wouldn't have seen it, since Ah Hin was facing away from them. "She took the treasures with her."

"Really?" said Little Brother sceptically.

"Yes," said Guet Imm.

She dropped on Little Brother's head, flicking the gun out of his hand. Both went down together in a confusion of robes and limbs, from which Ah Hin was ejected. He crashed into the undergrowth, crying out.

Tet Sang grabbed him, but, "I'm okay?" said Ah Hin, feeling himself for any injury. "I'm okay! Help sister!"

Ah Yee had vanished, but Tet Sang had no time to worry about that now. He wrenched the gun out of the nearest bandit's hand, kicking him in the stomach and using the gun to clock the next man over the head.

"Take that fellow's gun," Tet Sang said to Ah Hin. That was three bandits dealt with, including Little Brother, and one gun . . . "Where's your friend's weapon?"

While Ah Hin scrabbled around in the undergrowth, Tet Sang turned to check how Guet Imm was doing. She had managed to pin Little Brother to the ground.

"Bitch," gasped Little Brother. "The deity will punish you for betraying your Order!"

"Brother, you have misunderstood," said Guet Imm, with an extreme mildness that spoke of profound annoyance. "I *am* the Order—and all others like me." She looked up, meeting Tet Sang's eyes. "What do you think the deity bequeathed her relics to us for, if not for us to benefit?"

She was holding Little Brother's arms down, but she must have relaxed her grip briefly. He lunged out of her grasp and scooped up the gun Ah Hin had failed to find. He wriggled around, cocking the gun.

"Guet Imm!" shouted Tet Sang—too late, he thought, but time had taken on a curiously elastic quality. By rights, the gun should have gone off even as he yelled.

But Little Brother froze. As Tet Sang blinked, the gun went flying.

Guet Imm laid her hands on Little Brother's head, as gently as though she were giving him a blessing. There was a loud *crack*.

It was a sound Tet Sang had heard before—the unforgettable, final *crack* of a neck breaking. Ah Hin staggered back, his face grey with horror.

The bandits knew the sound too. There were two remaining on their feet. One turned and fled through the trees, but the other raised his gun, pointing it at the back of Guet Imm's head.

"Sister," gasped Ah Hin. He was cowering on the ground, so shaken his voice came out in a whisper. He tried again: "Sister!"

Tet Sang didn't waste his breath on trying to warn Guet Imm. He lunged, meaning to shove her out of the way of the bullet, but she disappeared even as he dived.

It was not that she moved quickly. She winked out of existence. Tet Sang rolled as he fell, managing to avoid Little Brother's corpse. Guet Imm reappeared behind the bandit who had tried to shoot her.

The bandit looked understandably startled. Tet Sang didn't see what Guet Imm did, but the bandit screamed, dropping his gun. The nun's hand flashed out, jabbing the bandit in the neck. His eyes rolled up and he slumped to the ground.

"Still got who else?" said Guet Imm. She wasn't even out of breath.

Tet Sang got to his feet. Little Brother was unmistakably dead. The two bandits Tet Sang had downed should be alive—he hadn't aimed to kill either—but if they were conscious, they had too much sense to betray it.

"There was one more fellow," Tet Sang began, when they heard the sound of running feet. Ah Hin tossed him one of the guns he'd got off the bandits, but it was Fung Cheung and Rimau who burst out of the trees.

"Ah Sang, how?" said Fung Cheung. He looked at the bandits strewn on the ground and lowered his parang.

"We're done for now," said Tet Sang. "Ah Yee came to find you?" Fung Cheung nodded. "The others?"

"Told them to go off first," said Fung Cheung. "We can catch up with them at— Shit."

He'd noticed Little Brother's corpse.

"Where's the fifth man?" said Guet Imm to Tet Sang.

Tet Sang jerked his head towards the approximate direction in which the bandit had gone. "Went off."

"So, he'll go and tell his brothers we killed one of their own?" said Fung Cheung. *"Shit!"*

"They know a nun killed him," said Guet Imm, speaking slowly and distinctly for the benefit of the bandits still living. "I am not part of your group. We are strangers who met on the road." She gave Tet Sang a pointed look.

"You killed him?" said Fung Cheung incredulously.

"Broke his neck," said Ah Hin. He looked at Guet Imm, woebegone. "Sister, you're a witch?"

It was more of a lament than a question. He did not really expect an answer, and Guet Imm gave none.

"What happened?" said Fung Cheung.

"I found sister," said Ah Hin. "But we just started talking only when the bandits ambushed us. She—" He waved his hands. "She disappeared! Just lenyap like that!"

"Sorry, brother," said Guet Imm. "I had to go keep the sarira away, make sure they were safe. I came back as soon as I could." She knelt by Ah Hin. "Are you hurt?"

But Ah Hin flinched away. Guet Imm's face went blank.

"If there was a survivor, the bandits will be coming

back," said Rimau to Fung Cheung. "We have to get out of here."

Guet Imm said, "You have time." She looked off into the trees, but there was a distant look in her eyes. It wasn't the trees she saw. "Their camp is not so close and the bandit is getting lost. He's not clever at navigating the jungle. It'll take him a while to get back to his camp."

Rimau and Fung Cheung exchanged a look.

"How do you know?" said Rimau.

"I can see it," said Guet Imm. She got up and dusted herself off. "The deity grants certain powers when there is need."

Her tone was matter of fact. Rimau and Ah Hin shifted, uneasy, but Fung Cheung was not superstitious. He looked irritated.

"If you could do magic all along, why didn't you defend yourself at the coffeehouse?" he demanded. "You could have just cursed that customer!"

"Brother has not been a waiter before, so you won't know," said Guet Imm. "But you're not supposed to curse your customers. You're supposed to serve them."

"The fight started in the first place because the customer said you hexed him!"

"He never proved it," said Guet Imm. "Anyway, *if* it happened, a small jampi to teach a man to keep his hands to himself is not the same as cursing that man to win a fight. Shaping the air is not for coffeehouse brawls. The deity lends us these powers so we can protect others, not for selfish purposes."

While Fung Cheung sputtered, Tet Sang said, "Those powers would have been useful at Sungai Tombak."

Guet Imm's face had been as smooth as the surface of still water, but this introduced a ripple. Her eyes dropped to Tet Sang's waist, where his wound was, under the bandages and robes.

"Yes," she admitted. "If I had known . . . but I was being careful. I was scared you all wouldn't understand."

She turned to Fung Cheung, bowing.

"Forgive me, brother. I've only been causing trouble since I joined you all," she said. "You should go now. Leave Kempas before the sun goes down and keep to the roads. You will be okay. The deity has shown me."

After a moment, Fung Cheung nodded. But Rimau was not a believer in the Tang deities.

"Even if we leave, where can we go?" he said. "The mata are chasing us. Now the bandits will be looking out for us also. There's nowhere on the peninsula where we will be safe."

"The bandits will be chasing me," said Guet Imm. It was a command, not a statement. She looked meaningfully at one of the bandits on the ground, who was blatantly observing the proceedings, having forgotten he was meant to be unconscious. He hastily shut his eyes and slumped.

"I'm the one who killed their brother," Guet Imm

continued. "And I'm the one who betrayed the Order, according to them. You are laypeople I misled. As for the mata . . ." She looked thoughtful. "Wait here first."

"Sister . . ." said Fung Cheung, but Guet Imm was no longer there. Fung Cheung looked around, stunned.

Even to Tet Sang, more used to wonders, it was startling—the abruptness with which Guet Imm was carved out of the world. At his tokong, there had been proficients in shaping the air, but they had not been encouraged to display their abilities where there was no need. The most he had seen was votaries levitating briefly while meditating; they had never got very far off the ground, and not for long. Guet Imm's gifts from the deity were on a different level.

He had assumed from her levity that she could not have been a very senior votary, though all anchorites were given a certain measure of deference, treated as a class above and apart. Madam Yeoh's failure to recognise her had seemed to confirm his assumption. But Guet Imm must have been a person of considerably more importance at her tokong than he had realised—so important that a transient acolyte like Yeoh Gaik Tin would not have been admitted to the secret of her powers.

Rimau was saying, "We should go," when Guet Imm reappeared next to Fung Cheung. He jumped.

"There," said Guet Imm. She was holding out a bag in which the sarira gleamed. "Go to Madam Yeoh before you leave Kempas, and collect the balance. If you ask her for help, I think you won't have so much trouble with the mata. But even if she decides not to help, you can bribe the mata with the cash."

Fung Cheung took the bag from her hand with care. All three men—Fung Cheung, Rimau and Ah Hin— were looking at Guet Imm as though she might hit them with a jampi if they made any sudden moves.

"And you?" said Fung Cheung.

"I'll draw the bandits off your track," said Guet Imm absently. She looked distrait, as if, having cut herself off from the group, she had already departed in spirit. "Don't worry about me."

Fung Cheung hesitated. For one who, like Tet Sang, had known him for so long, his feelings were transparently inscribed on his face—relief that Guet Imm was proposing to solve the problem of herself and the bandits in one go, but also a sense of obligation, a debt incurred. It would have suited Fung Cheung better to have deposited the nun at Yeoh Gaik Tin's house—he would have felt then that she was properly settled.

Sure enough, after a pause, Fung Cheung said, "You don't want to take up Madam Yeoh's offer, sister? A safe haven is nothing to sniff at in these times."

Guet Imm smiled faintly. It didn't reach her eyes. "That was Brother Tet Sang's idea." She didn't look at Tet Sang. "His intentions were good, but I am not qualified to be a rich woman's tame priestess. You see, I was an anchorite at my tokong. You don't go into seclusion because you are good at respecting authority. Brother Tet Sang will be able to explain."

"No," said Tet Sang, "because I'm coming with you."

He hadn't known what he was going to say before he spoke, but once the words were out, peace settled on him. His path was clear. He had not felt such certainty since he had left the tokong at Permatang Timbul.

"Wait, what?" said Fung Cheung.

"Second Brother!" said Ah Hin.

The blood drained from Guet Imm's face. Then it rushed back and she went a brilliant red. "What do you mean, 'coming with me'?"

"I mean, I am going to leave the group and follow you," said Tet Sang, enunciating so as to avoid any possibility of a misunderstanding.

"But you can't," said Guet Imm. "You have to stay with the brothers."

"That's right," said Ah Hin. "You have to stay with us!"

Tet Sang was gazing at Guet Imm, but he spoke to Ah Hin.

"I am not under any contract," said Tet Sang. "There's nothing to say I must stay here or go there. You were fine before I joined you all, and you'll be fine without me." He paused. "Of course, it depends on whether Sister Guet Imm minds if I come with her or not."

"What are you talking about?" said Guet Imm. "You're the one who wanted to get rid of me!"

"It would have been good for you to stay with Madam Yeoh," said Tet Sang. "If you could take it." He shrugged. "It was a wrong decision. I'm sorry, sister. I should have asked first. Do you want me, or should I stay with Ah Lau and the brothers?"

"Want you!" said Guet Imm peevishly. "Do you have to ask?"

Ah Hin turned to Fung Cheung. "Big Brother, say something!"

"You're not going to let this happen, Cheung?" said Rimau.

Fung Cheung looked from Tet Sang to Guet Imm. He whistled. "Oh, it's like that, is it?" He didn't sound surprised.

Neither Tet Sang nor Guet Imm was paying any attention to the others.

"You'll regret it in time," said Guet Imm. "You'll start scolding me . . ."

"Regret for what? If it doesn't work out, then we go our separate ways," said Tet Sang. "Nobody is swearing any oaths. But if you're hoping I won't scold you, then I better not come."

Guet Imm tossed her head. "Oh, even I am not so hopeful, brother!"

"So, you're going?" said Fung Cheung.

Tet Sang tore his eyes away from Guet Imm. "Sorry, Ah Lau." There was too much to say—and yet there was no need to say anything. Everything of importance had always been understood between him and Fung Cheung.

But then Tet Sang remembered that there was a small matter worth mentioning.

"There'll be more money to divide between everybody," he said.

This consideration had evidently not occurred to Rimau and Ah Hin till now. They perked up at once. Only Fung Cheung seemed to derive little comfort from it.

"You told me not to take her on. Should have listened to you from the start," he said. "If I knew this was going to happen, I would never have let sister join the group. No offence, sister."

"None taken," said Guet Imm.

Tet Sang had gone back to looking at her, and she was looking at him. A strange thought came to him, less painful than it should have been.

"I might never have met you if they didn't burn the tokong," he said. He meant his own tokong, but of course, it was equally true of hers.

"Ah!" said Guet Imm softly. "Don't talk like that. You will make me glad of things I must regret."

This was all deeply meaningful and of enormous interest to both of them, so neither was prepared when Fung Cheung seized Tet Sang's face and kissed him.

Fung Cheung had ability as well as enthusiasm, but it was probably not the most successful of his kisses. Tet Sang gaped. He could hear a loud hissing, as from an enraged snake.

Fung Cheung let him go, laughing. Guet Imm, who proved to be the hisser, grabbed Tet Sang's arm and yanked him away.

Fung Cheung put his hands together. "I had to try it once, sister. Don't hurt me! You members of the elect must have compassion on us lower beings."

"Try it again and I'll cut your balls off!" snarled Guet Imm.

"Guet Imm," said Tet Sang, but this made her turn on him.

"You didn't believe me when I said Brother Lau liked you! Piece of wood, you said. Now you see!"

"Why are you angry at me?" said Tet Sang, starting to get annoyed. "I didn't ask him to kiss me also!"

"You two already fight like husband and wife," said Fung Cheung. "I should have seen it coming." He shook his head, then put his hand into his robes and drew out a purse, offering it to Tet Sang.

"What's this?" said Tet Sang, conscious of Ah Hin and Rimau's eyes on him.

"Money. Not your full share," added Fung Cheung. "Only about one hundred cash. The rest we will keep, don't worry."

"You don't need to give me anything."

"Don't fight, Ah Sang," said Fung Cheung. "If I'm feeling like being generous, you should give me face. It's not so often I'm in the mood to gain pahala."

"Don't do me any favours, Ah Lau," Tet Sang began, but Guet Imm cut off the brewing argument by reaching out and plucking the bag from Fung Cheung's hand.

"Thank you, brother," she said.

"At least one of you is sensible," said Fung Cheung. "Now I'll worry less."

Rimau cleared his throat.

"Cheung," he said. "We should make a move."

Fung Cheung nodded without taking his eyes off Tet Sang.

"Go slowly, brother," he said.

"Go slowly," said Tet Sang.

ACKNOWLEDGMENTS

Thank you to my editor Jonathan Strahan for shaking me until a novella fell out; my agent Caitlin Blasdell for making sure the shaking wasn't too violent; Hana Lee and Tony Tonnu for the helpful beta; Sija Hong for the brilliant cover illustration and Sarah J. Coleman for the lettering; and the Tor.com Publishing team for bringing this book into the world: Ruoxi Chen, Irene Gallo, Christine Foltzer, Caroline Perny, Mordicai Knode, Amanda Melfi, Jamie-Lee Nardone, Lauren Hougen, and Richard Shealy.

As always, both I and my book benefited hugely from the support of my family, especially my mom and dad; my in-laws, Martin and Bernadette; and my husband, Peter. Finally, I would like to thank Teddy for delaying his arrival in the world for just long enough so I could complete the first draft.

This book is dedicated to Rachel Monte, in memory of a certain Millefeuille of Destiny.